THE RETURN OF
THE SMURFETTE

Peyo

THE RETURN OF THE SMURFETTE

I'll have to resmurf my "Serenade to the Smurfette"!
You, o you, my Smurfette what rhymes with Smurfette?
Ah dear me, I can sense I'll be dreaming about Smurfette!
That night...
Pellet, marionette, barrette...
...and stick it in the oven!
Toot! PWAAA!
ZZZ
And the next day...
Don't smurf! I was here first!
Who? You? Yes, my smurf! I was!
THERE SHE IS!
Yoohoo! Hello, hello!

A SMURFS GRAPHIC NOVEL BY Peyo

PAPERCUTZ™
NEW YORK

SMURFS GRAPHIC NOVELS AVAILABLE FROM PAPERCUTZ™

1. **THE PURPLE SMURFS**
2. **THE SMURFS AND THE MAGIC FLUTE**
3. **THE SMURF KING**
4. **THE SMURFETTE**
5. **THE SMURFS AND THE EGG**
6. **THE SMURFS AND THE HOWLIBIRD**
7. **THE ASTROSMURF**
8. **THE SMURF APPRENTICE**
9. **GARGAMEL AND THE SMURFS**
10. **THE RETURN OF THE SMURFETTE**
11. **THE SMURF OLYMPICS**
12. **SMURF VS. SMURF**
13. **SMURF SOUP**
14. **THE BABY SMURF**
15. **THE SMURFLINGS**
16. **THE AEROSMURF**

COMING SOON:

17. **THE STRANGE AWAKENING OF LAZY SMURF**

THE SMURFS graphic novels are available in paperback for $5.99 each and in hardcover for $10.99 each at booksellers everywhere. You can also order online at www.papercutz.com. Or call 1-800-886-1223, Monday through Friday, 9 – 5 EST. MC, Visa, and AmEx accepted. To order by mail, please add $4.00 for postage and handling for first book ordered, $1.00 for each additional book and make check payable to NBM Publishing. Send to: Papercutz, 160 Broadway, Suite 700, East Wing, New York, NY 10038.

THE SMURFS graphic novels are also available digitally wherever e-books are sold.

PAPERCUTZ.COM

THE RETURN OF THE SMURFETTE ♥

SMURF™ © Peyo ™ - 2012 - Licensed through Lafig Belgium - www.smurf.com

"Romeos and Smurfette"
BY YVAN DELPORTE AND PEYO

"The Return of the Smurfette"
BY YVAN DELPORTE AND PEYO

"The Smurf Garden"
BY PEYO

"The Handy Smurf"
BY PEYO

"Halloween"
BY PEYO

"Smurferies"
BY PEYO

Joe Johnson, SMURFLATIONS
Adam Grano, SMURFIC DESIGN
Janice Chiang, LETTERING SMURFETTE
Diego Jourdan, PURPLE SMURFILIZATION
Matt. Murray, SMURF CONSULTANT
Beth Scorzato, SMURF COORDINATOR
Michael Petranek, ASSOCIATE SMURF
Jim Salicrup, SMURF-IN-CHIEF

PAPERBACK EDITION ISBN: 978-1-59707-292-2
HARDCOVER EDITION ISBN: 978-1-59707-293-9

PRINTED IN THE US JUNE 2013 BY LIFETOUCH PRINTING
5126 FOREST HILLS CT.
LOVES PARK, IL 61111

Papercutz books may be purchased for business or
promotional use. For information on bulk purchases
please contact Macmillan Corporate and Premium
Sales Department at (800) 221-7945 x5442.

DISTRIBUTED BY MACMILLAN
SECOND PAPERCUTZ PRINTING

ROMEOS
AND
SMURFETTE

A hundred Smurfs were living in peace.
A Smurfette came along
But that's another story.[1]

You were wondering what became of her.
She's doing well.
From time to time, she comes back to the village, and
As these stories will show, she hasn't changed.

Peyo ✳ *Y. Delporte*

[1] A story told in SMURFS #4 "The Smurfette."

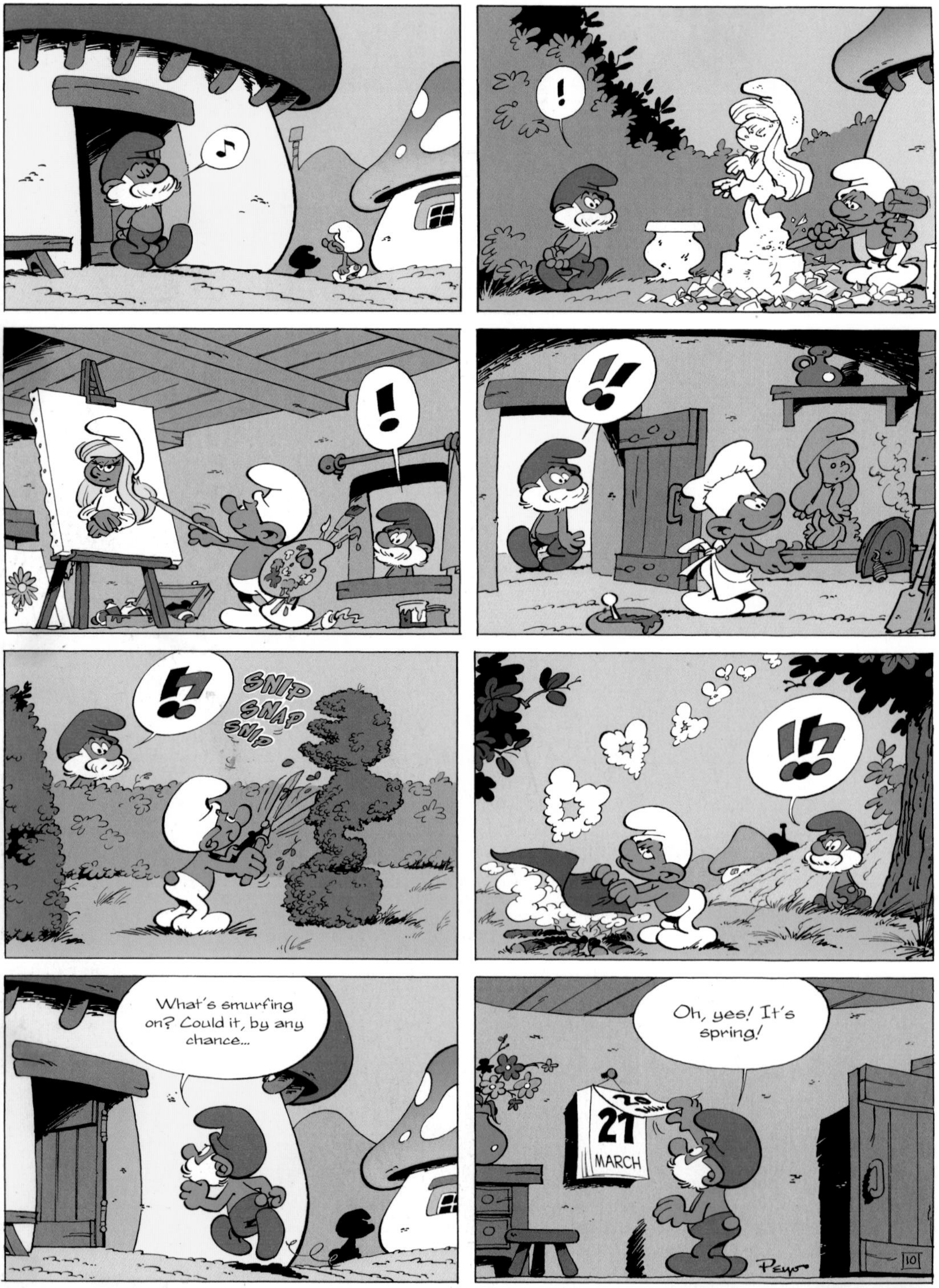
!
!
SNIP
SNAP
SNIP
What's smurfing on? Could it, by any chance...
Oh, yes! It's spring!
21
MARCH

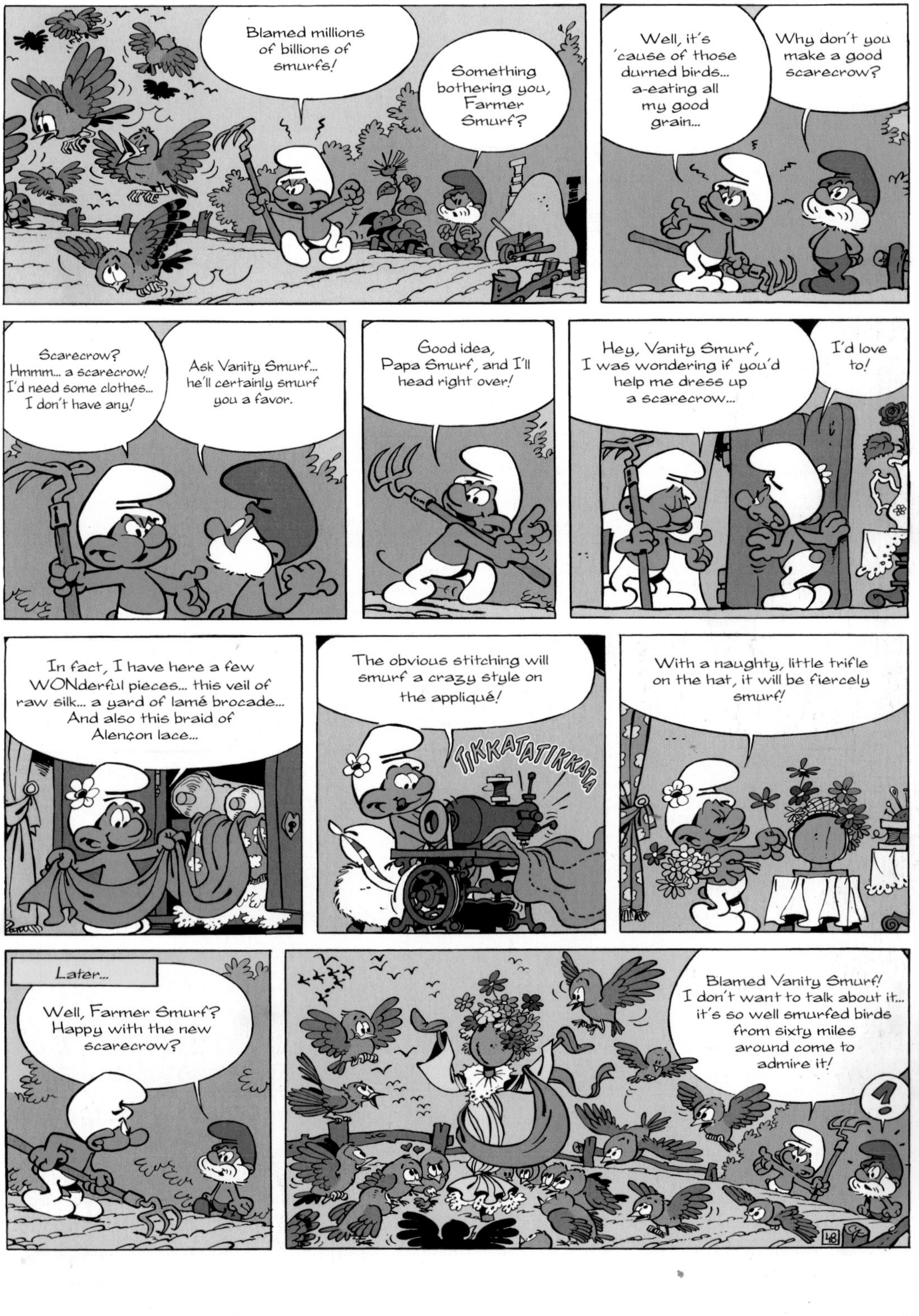

Blamed millions of billions of smurfs!
Something bothering you, Farmer Smurf?
Well, it's 'cause of those durned birds... a-eating all my good grain...
Why don't you make a good scarecrow?
Scarecrow? Hmmm... a scarecrow! I'd need some clothes... I don't have any!
Ask Vanity Smurf... he'll certainly smurf you a favor.
Good idea, Papa Smurf, and I'll head right over!
Hey, Vanity Smurf, I was wondering if you'd help me dress up a scarecrow...
I'd love to!
In fact, I have here a few WONderful pieces... this veil of raw silk... a yard of lamé brocade... And also this braid of Alençon lace...
The obvious stitching will smurf a crazy style on the appliqué!
TIKKATATIKKATA
With a naughty, little trifle on the hat, it will be fiercely smurf!
Later...
Well, Farmer Smurf? Happy with the new scarecrow?
Blamed Vanity Smurf! I don't want to talk about it... it's so well smurfed birds from sixty miles around come to admire it!
?

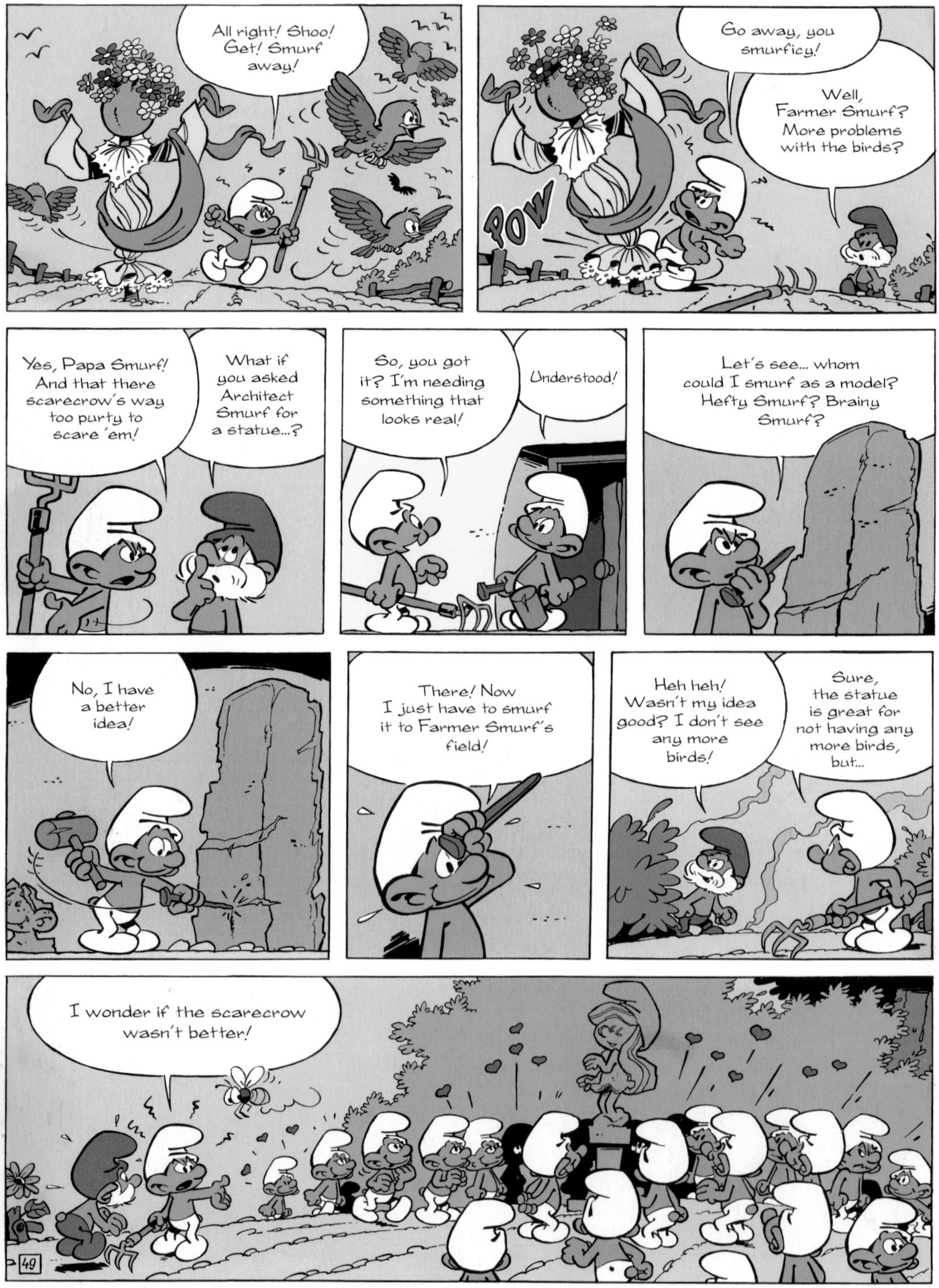
All right! Shoo! Get! Smurf away!
Go away, you smurficy!
POW
Well, Farmer Smurf? More problems with the birds?
Yes, Papa Smurf! And that there scarecrow's way too purty to scare 'em!
What if you asked Architect Smurf for a statue...?
So, you got it? I'm needing something that looks real!
Understood!
Let's see... whom could I smurf as a model? Hefty Smurf? Brainy Smurf?
No, I have a better idea!
There! Now I just have to smurf it to Farmer Smurf's field!
Heh heh! Wasn't my idea good? I don't see any more birds!
Sure, the statue is great for not having any more birds, but...
I wonder if the scarecrow wasn't better!
49

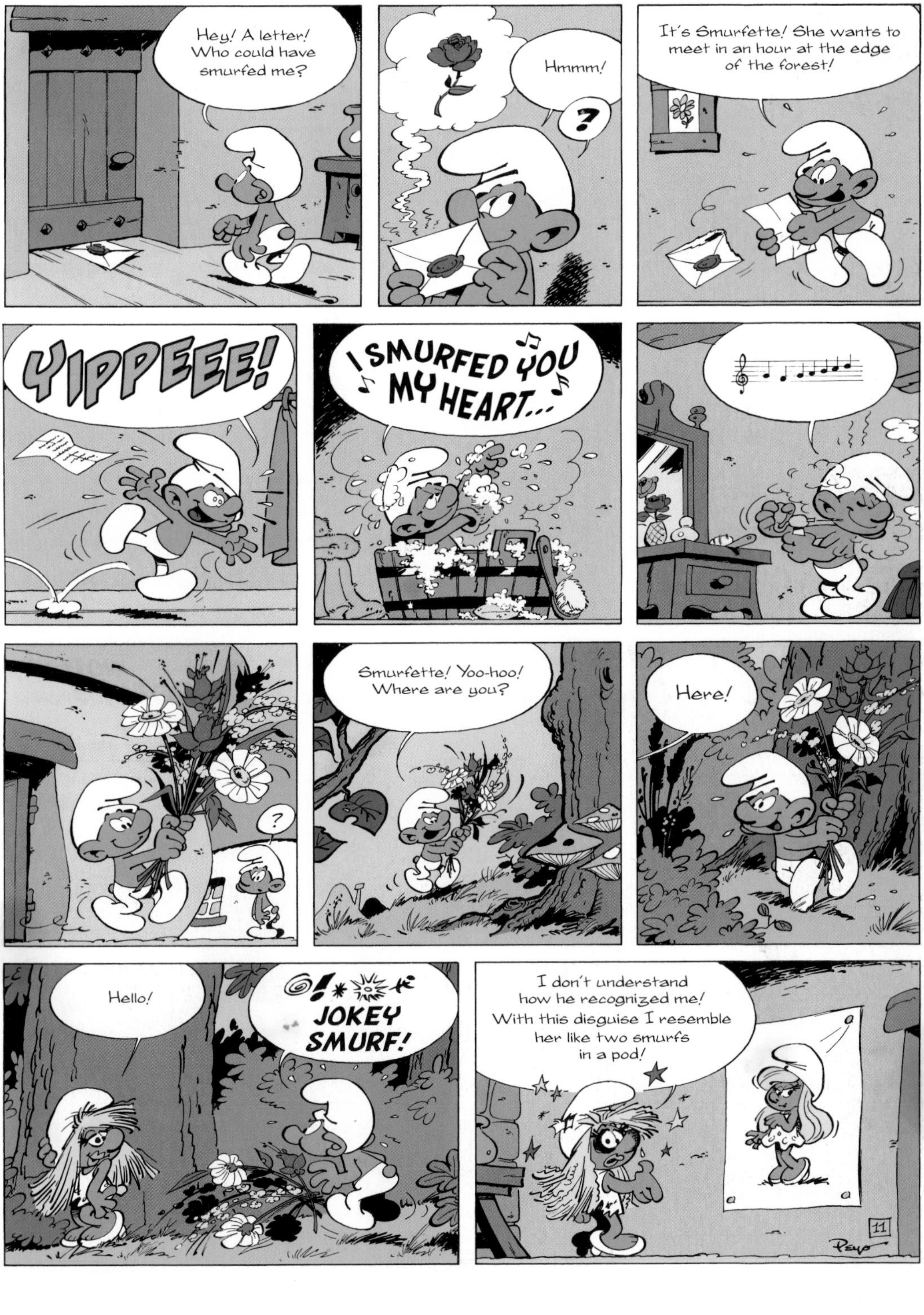
Hey! A letter! Who could have smurfed me?
Hmmm!
?
It's Smurfette! She wants to meet in an hour at the edge of the forest!
YIPPEEE!
I SMURFED YOU MY HEART...
?
Smurfette! Yoo-hoo! Where are you?
Here!
Hello!
JOKEY SMURF!
I don't understand how he recognized me! With this disguise I resemble her like two smurfs in a pod!
11
Peyo

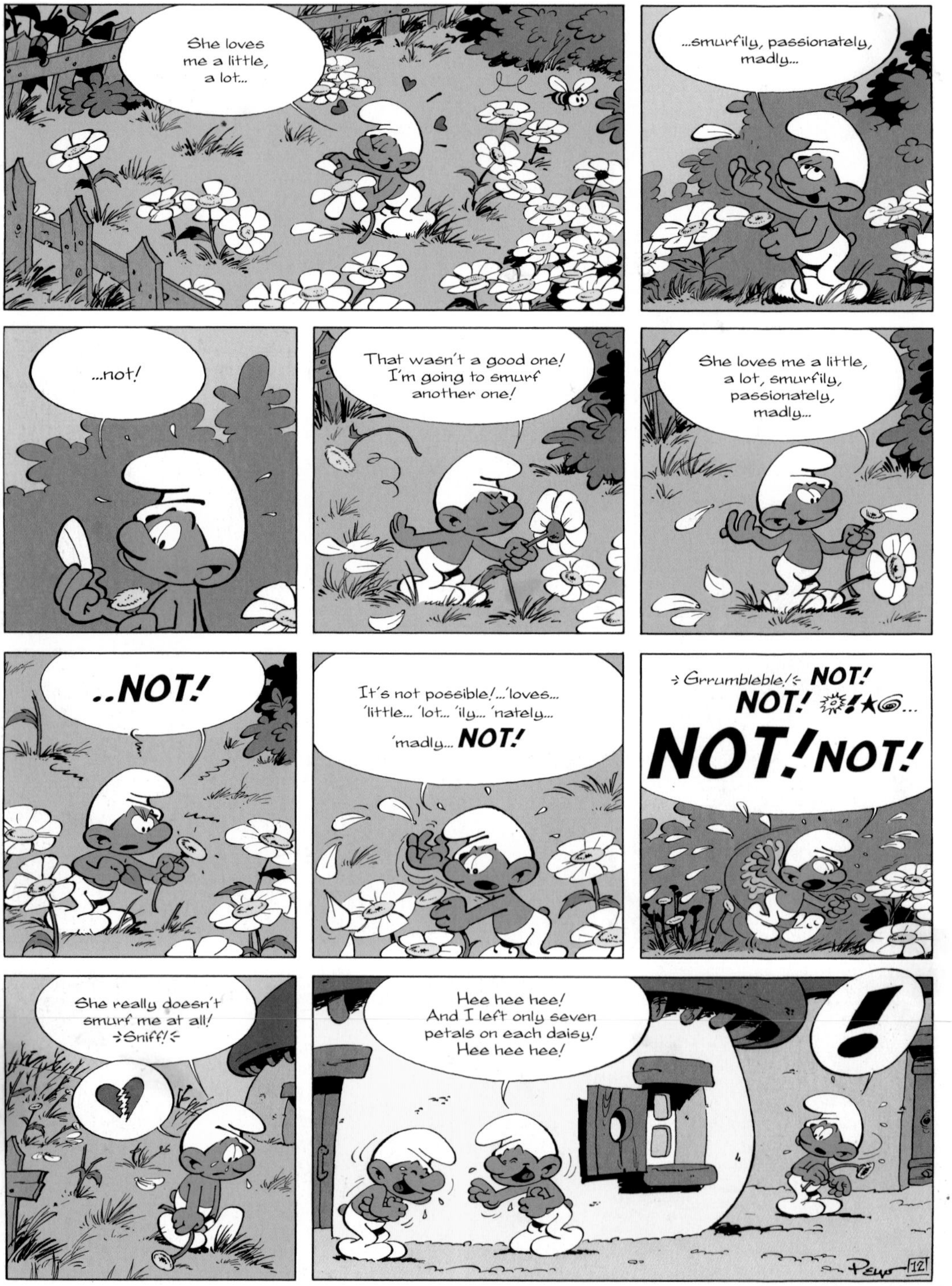

She loves me a little, a lot...
...smurfily, passionately, madly...
...not!
That wasn't a good one! I'm going to smurf another one!
She loves me a little, a lot, smurfily, passionately, madly...
..NOT!
It's not possible!...'loves... 'little... 'lot... 'ily... 'nately... 'madly... NOT!
Grrumbleble! NOT! NOT! ... NOT! NOT!
She really doesn't smurf me at all! Sniff!
Hee hee hee! And I left only seven petals on each daisy! Hee hee hee!
!

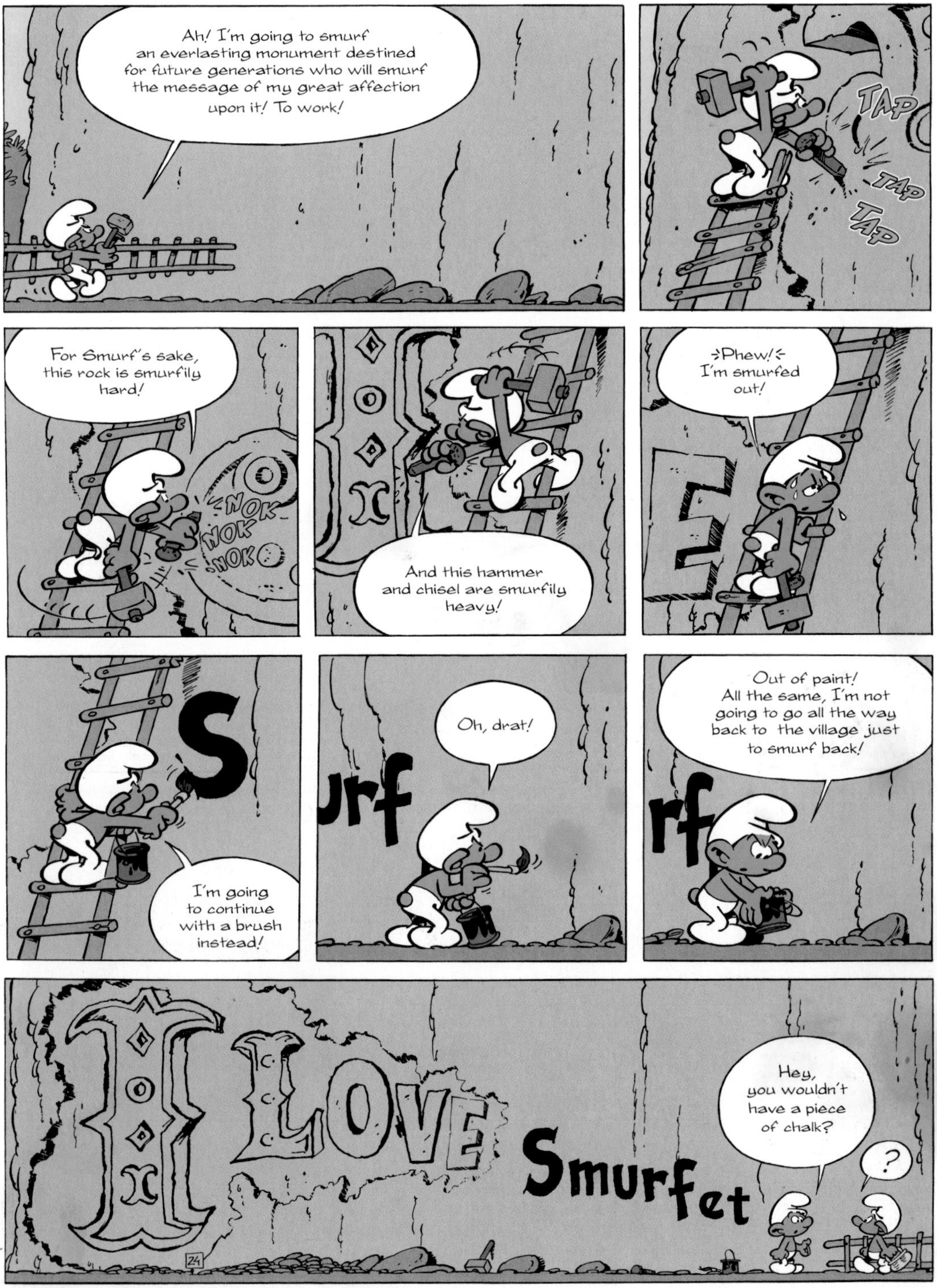

Ah! I'm going to smurf an everlasting monument destined for future generations who will smurf the message of my great affection upon it! To work!
TAP
TAP
TAP
For Smurf's sake, this rock is smurfily hard!
NOK
NOK
NOK
And this hammer and chisel are smurfily heavy!
Phew! I'm smurfed out!
S
I'm going to continue with a brush instead!
urf
Oh, drat!
rf
Out of paint! All the same, I'm not going to go all the way back to the village just to smurf back!
I LOVE Smurfet
Hey, you wouldn't have a piece of chalk?
?
24

THE RETURN OF THE SMURFETTE

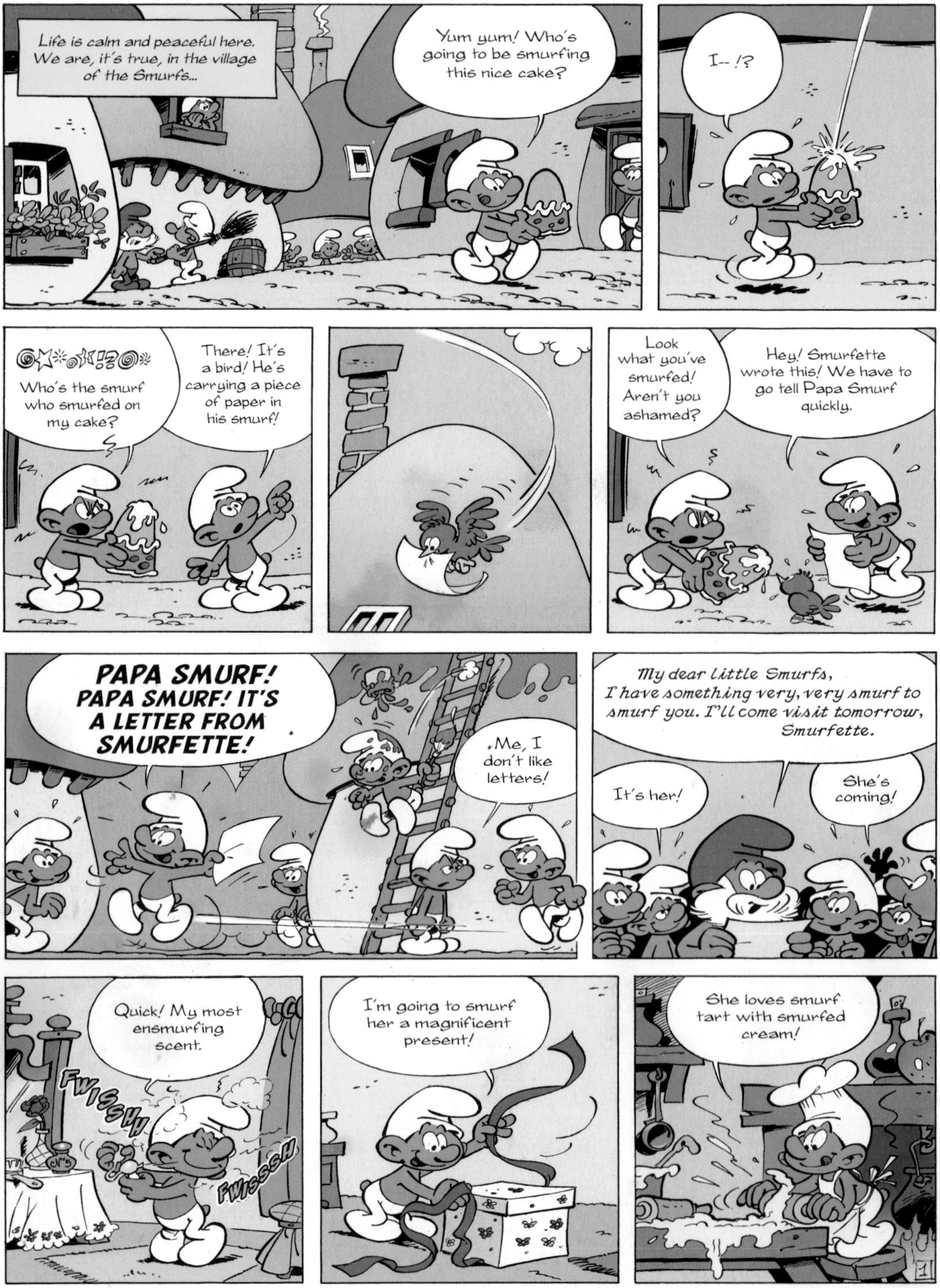

Life is calm and peaceful here. We are, it's true, in the village of the Smurfs...
Yum yum! Who's going to be smurfing this nice cake?
I-- !?
Who's the smurf who smurfed on my cake?
There! It's a bird! He's carrying a piece of paper in his smurf!
Look what you've smurfed! Aren't you ashamed?
Hey! Smurfette wrote this! We have to go tell Papa Smurf quickly.
PAPA SMURF! PAPA SMURF! IT'S A LETTER FROM SMURFETTE!
Me, I don't like letters!
My dear little Smurfs, I have something very, very smurf to smurf you. I'll come visit tomorrow, Smurfette.
It's her!
She's coming!
Quick! My most ensmurfing scent.
FWISSHH
FWISSSH
I'm going to smurf her a magnificent present!
She loves smurf tart with smurfed cream!
1

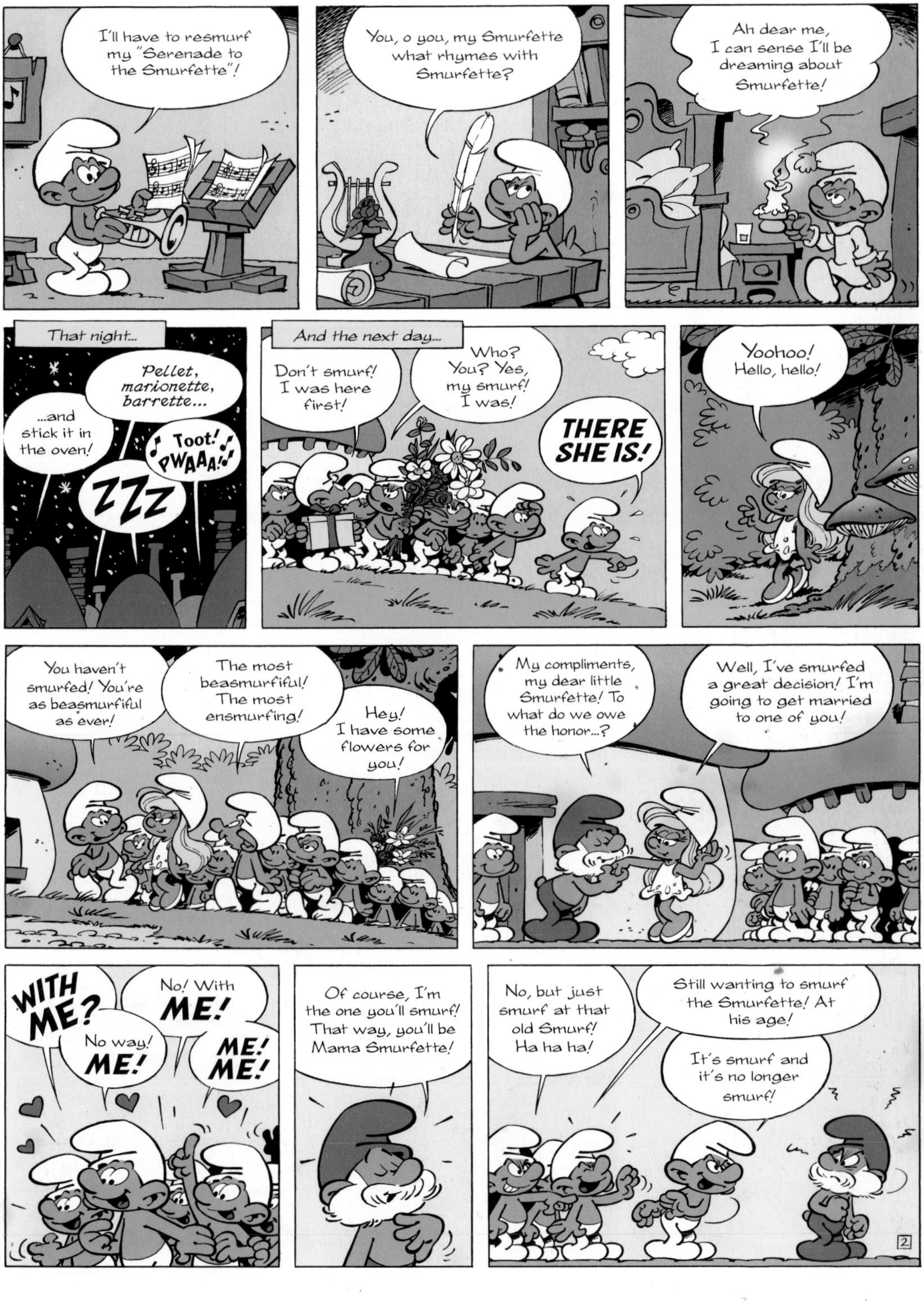
I'll have to resmurf my "Serenade to the Smurfette"!
You, o you, my Smurfette what rhymes with Smurfette?
Ah dear me, I can sense I'll be dreaming about Smurfette!
That night...
...and stick it in the oven!
Pellet, marionette, barrette...
ZZZ
Toot! PWAAA!
And the next day...
Don't smurf! I was here first!
Who? You? Yes, my smurf! I was!
THERE SHE IS!
Yoohoo! Hello, hello!
You haven't smurfed! You're as beasmurfiful as ever!
The most beasmurfiful! The most ensmurfing!
Hey! I have some flowers for you!
My compliments, my dear little Smurfette! To what do we owe the honor...?
Well, I've smurfed a great decision! I'm going to get married to one of you!
WITH ME?
No! With ME!
No way! ME!
ME! ME!
Of course, I'm the one you'll smurf! That way, you'll be Mama Smurfette!
No, but just smurf at that old Smurf! Ha ha ha!
Still wanting to smurf the Smurfette! At his age!
It's smurf and it's no longer smurf!
2

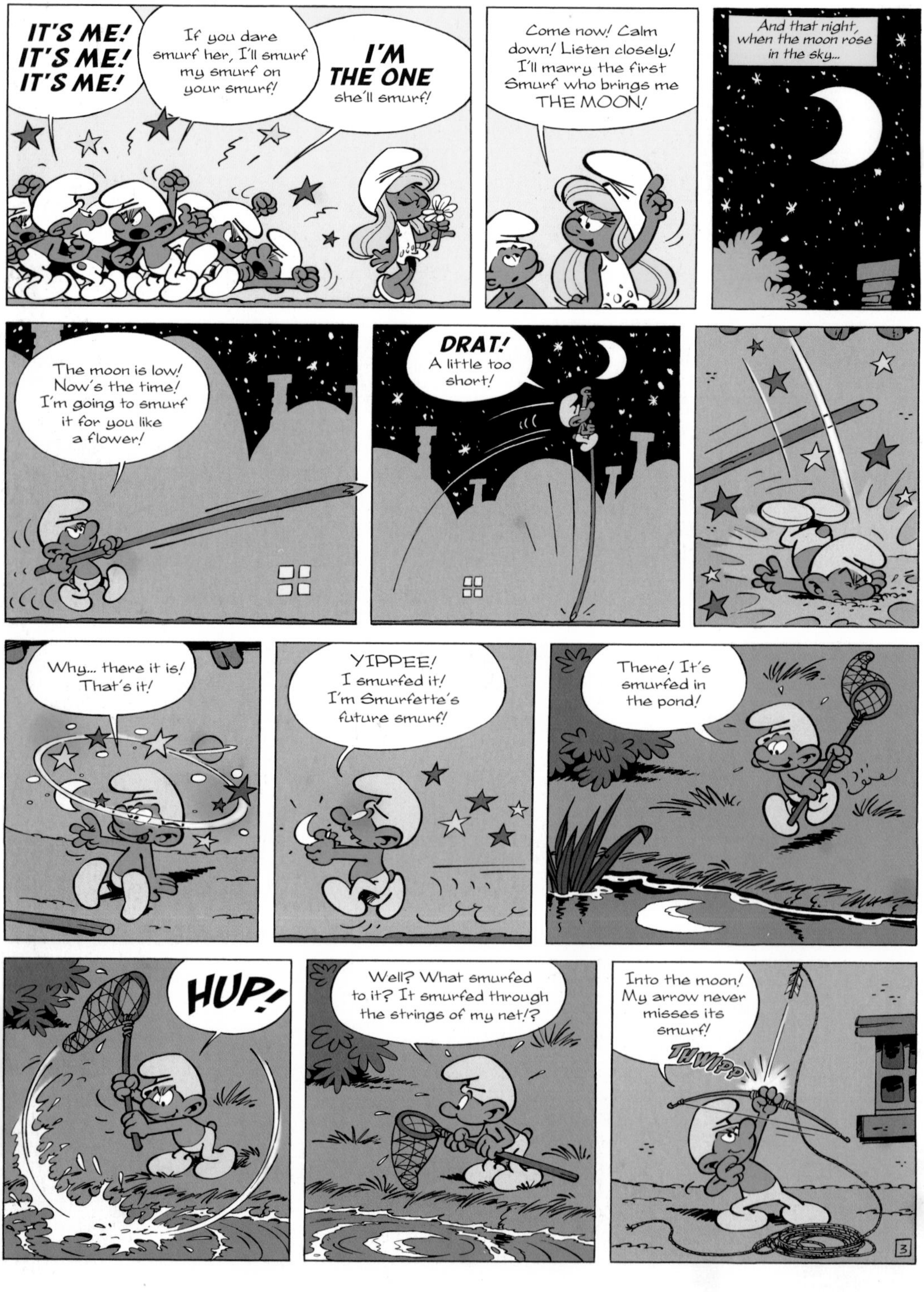
IT'S ME! IT'S ME! IT'S ME!
If you dare smurf her, I'll smurf my smurf on your smurf!
I'M THE ONE she'll smurf!
Come now! Calm down! Listen closely! I'll marry the first Smurf who brings me THE MOON!
And that night, when the moon rose in the sky...
The moon is low! Now's the time! I'm going to smurf it for you like a flower!
DRAT! A little too short!
Why... there it is! That's it!
YIPPEE! I smurfed it! I'm Smurfette's future smurf!
There! It's smurfed in the pond!
HUP!
Well? What smurfed to it? It smurfed through the strings of my net!?
Into the moon! My arrow never misses its smurf!
THWIPP
3

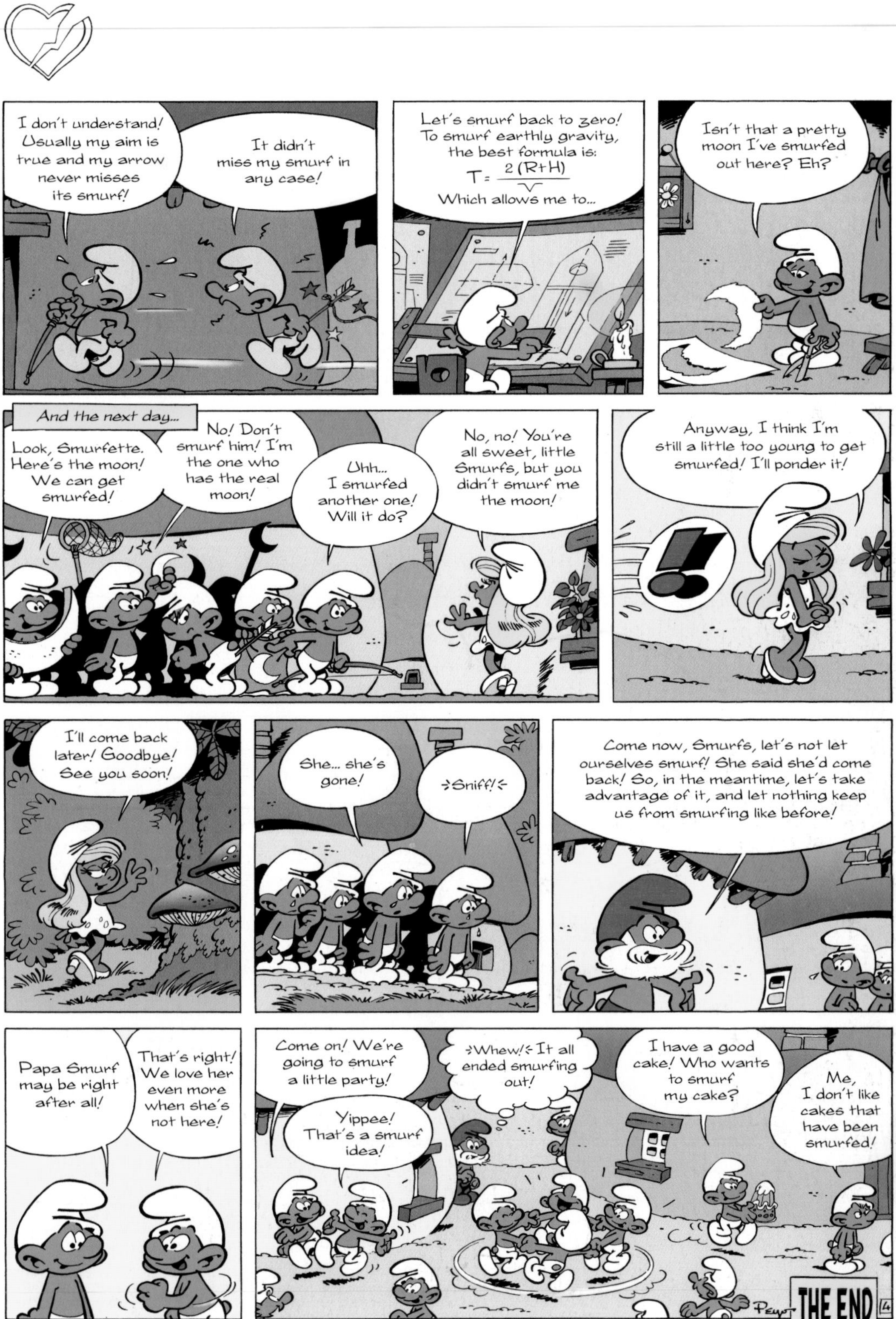
I don't understand! Usually my aim is true and my arrow never misses its smurf!
It didn't miss my smurf in any case!
Let's smurf back to zero! To smurf earthly gravity, the best formula is: T = 2 (R+H) / √ Which allows me to...
Isn't that a pretty moon I've smurfed out here? Eh?
And the next day...
Look, Smurfette. Here's the moon! We can get smurfed!
No! Don't smurf him! I'm the one who has the real moon!
Uhh... I smurfed another one! Will it do?
No, no! You're all sweet, little Smurfs, but you didn't smurf me the moon!
Anyway, I think I'm still a little too young to get smurfed! I'll ponder it!
I'll come back later! Goodbye! See you soon!
She... she's gone!
Sniff!
Come now, Smurfs, let's not let ourselves smurf! She said she'd come back! So, in the meantime, let's take advantage of it, and let nothing keep us from smurfing like before!
Papa Smurf may be right after all!
That's right! We love her even more when she's not here!
Come on! We're going to smurf a little party!
Yippee! That's a smurf idea!
Whew! It all ended smurfing out!
I have a good cake! Who wants to smurf my cake?
Me, I don't like cakes that have been smurfed!
Peyo
THE END
4

THE SMURF GARDEN

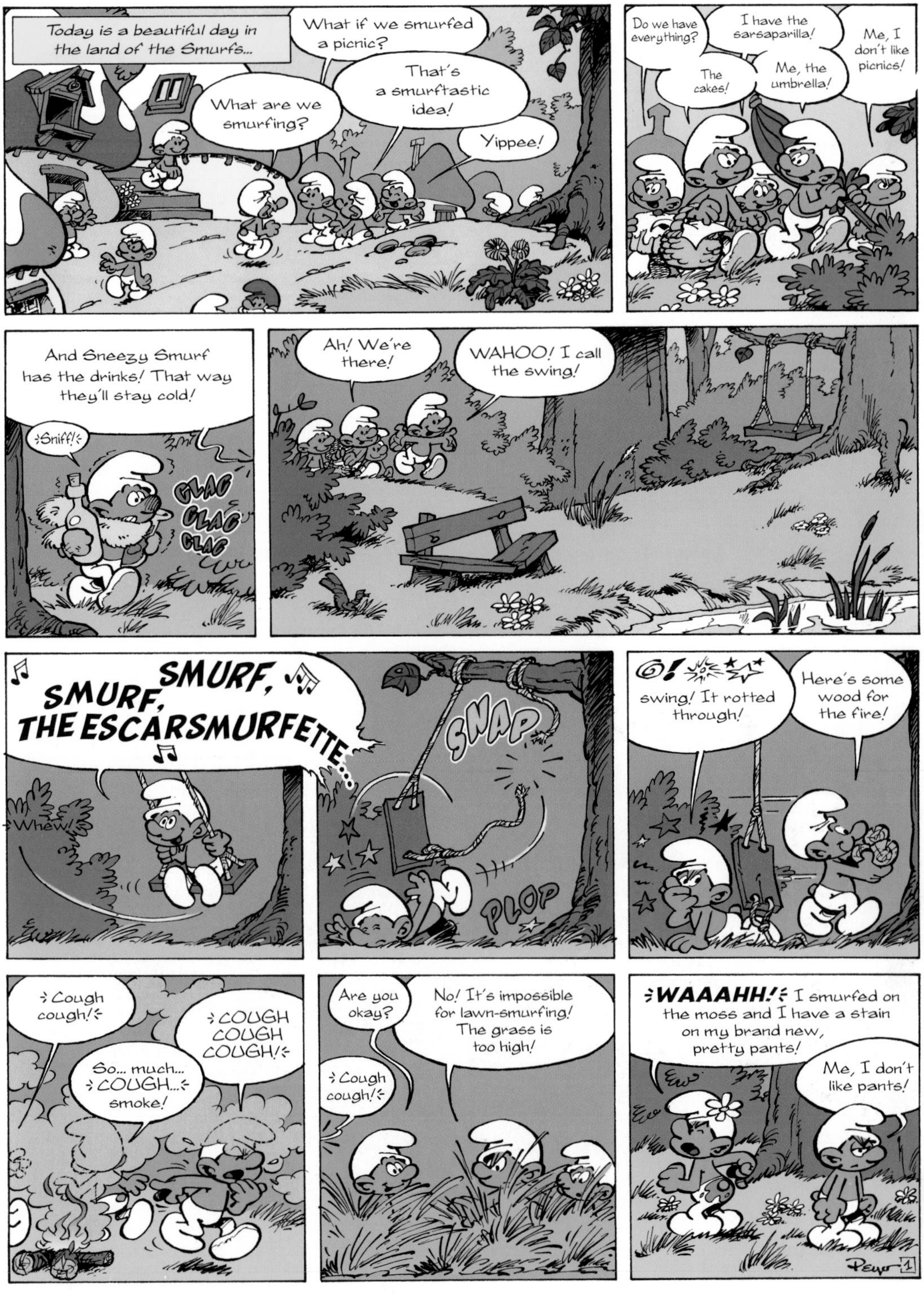

Today is a beautiful day in the land of the Smurfs...
What if we smurfed a picnic?
What are we smurfing?
That's a smurftastic idea!
Yippee!
Do we have everything?
I have the sarsaparilla!
Me, I don't like picnics!
The cakes!
Me, the umbrella!
And Sneezy Smurf has the drinks! That way they'll stay cold!
Sniff!
CLAG CLAG CLAG
Ah! We're there!
WAHOO! I call the swing!
SMURF, SMURF, THE ESCARSMURFETTE...
Whew!
SNAP
PLOP
swing! It rotted through!
Here's some wood for the fire!
Cough cough!
COUGH COUGH COUGH!
So... much... COUGH... smoke!
Are you okay?
No! It's impossible for lawn-smurfing! The grass is too high!
Cough cough!
WAAAHH! I smurfed on the moss and I have a stain on my brand new, pretty pants!
Me, I don't like pants!

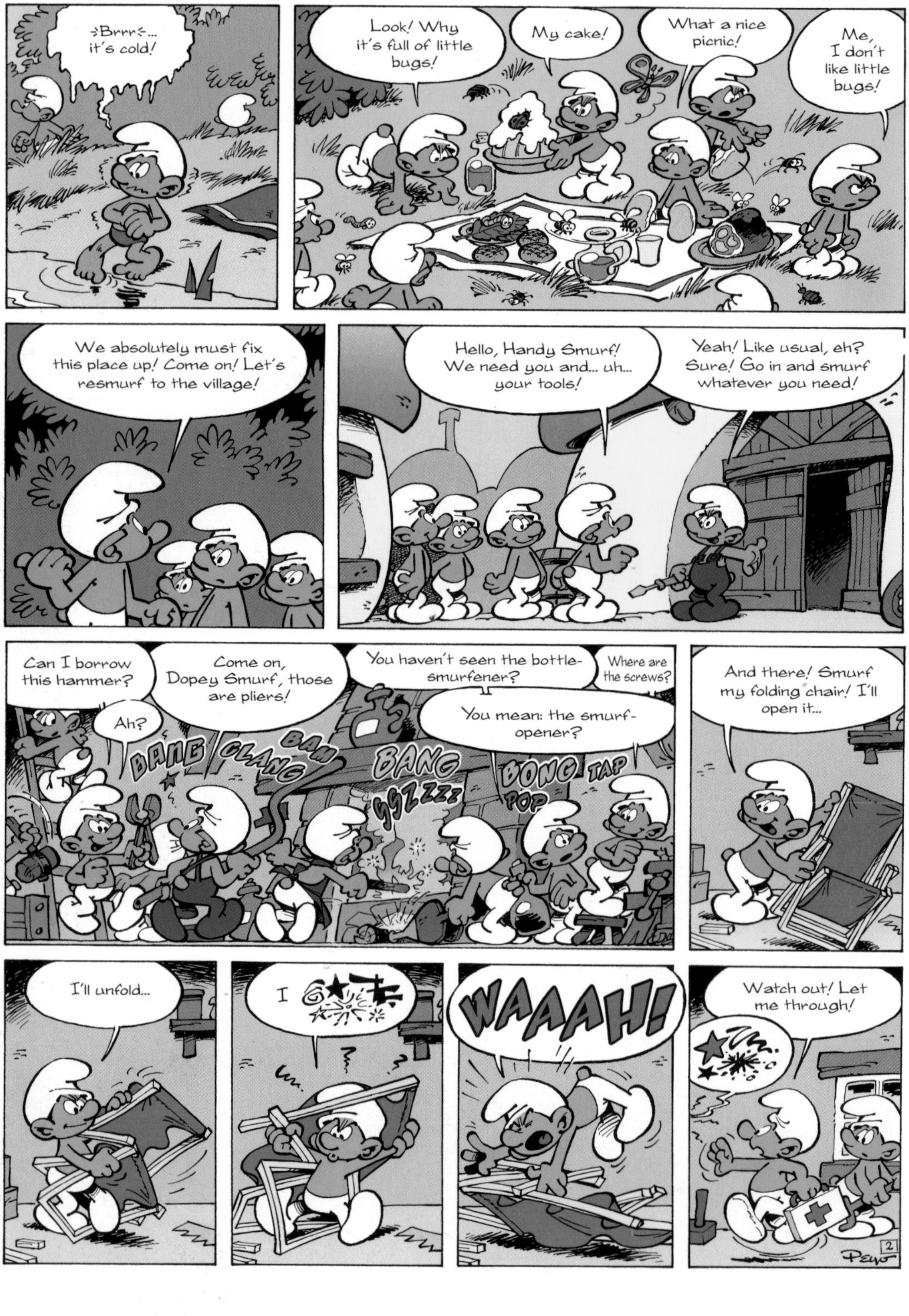
Brrr... it's cold!
Look! Why it's full of little bugs!
My cake!
What a nice picnic!
Me, I don't like little bugs!
We absolutely must fix this place up! Come on! Let's resmurf to the village!
Hello, Handy Smurf! We need you and... uh... your tools!
Yeah! Like usual, eh? Sure! Go in and smurf whatever you need!
Can I borrow this hammer?
Come on, Dopey Smurf, those are pliers!
Ah?
You haven't seen the bottle-smurfener?
Where are the screws?
You mean: the smurf-opener?
BANG CLANG BAM BANG BONG TAP POP
And there! Smurf my folding chair! I'll open it...
I'll unfold...
I
WAAAH!
Watch out! Let me through!
Peyo

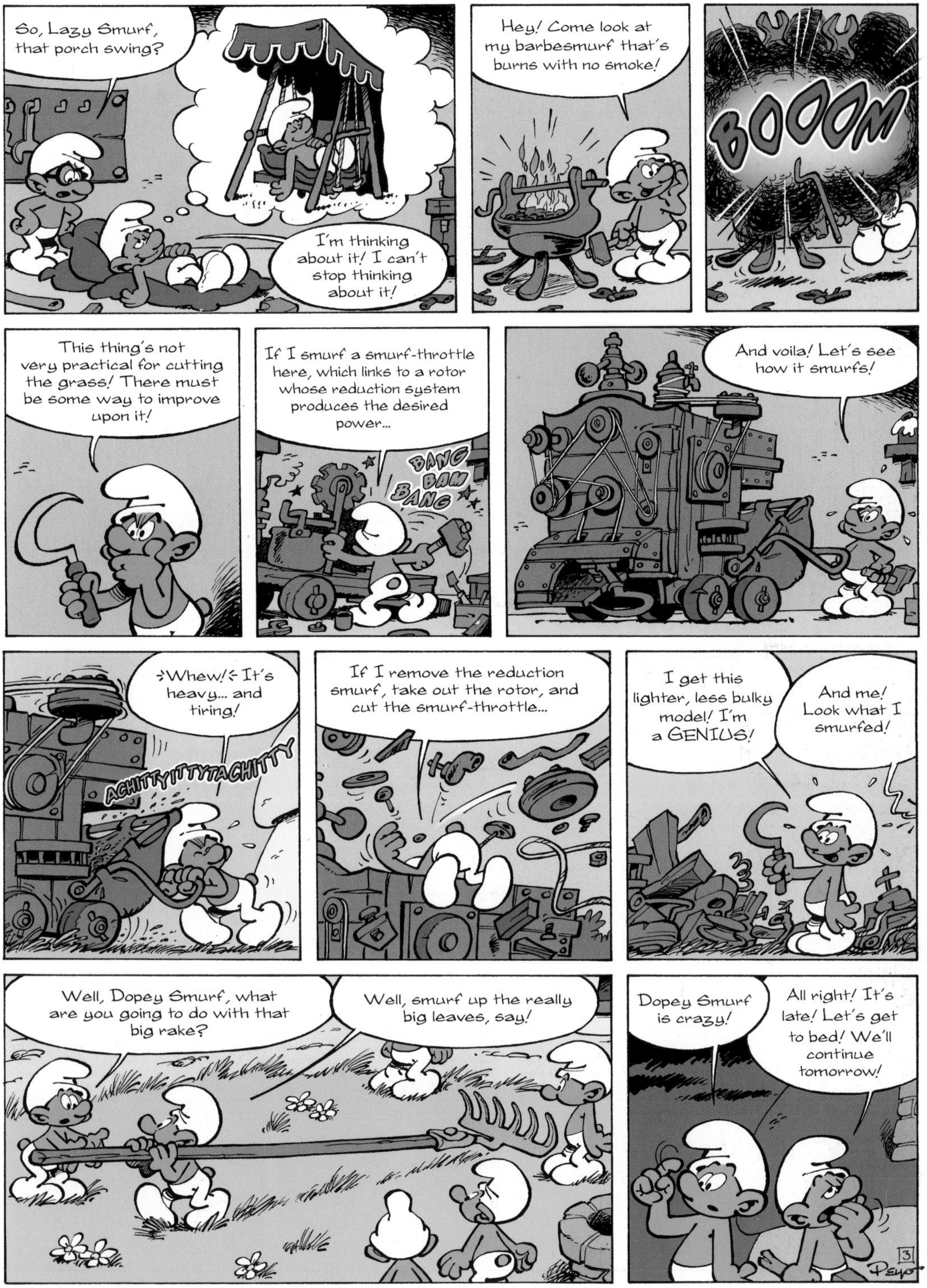
So, Lazy Smurf, that porch swing?
I'm thinking about it! I can't stop thinking about it!
Hey! Come look at my barbesmurf that's burns with no smoke!
BOOOM
This thing's not very practical for cutting the grass! There must be some way to improve upon it!
If I smurf a smurf-throttle here, which links to a rotor whose reduction system produces the desired power...
BANG BAM BANG
And voila! Let's see how it smurfs!
Whew! It's heavy... and tiring!
ACHITTYITTYTACHITTY
If I remove the reduction smurf, take out the rotor, and cut the smurf-throttle...
I get this lighter, less bulky model! I'm a GENIUS!
And me! Look what I smurfed!
Well, Dopey Smurf, what are you going to do with that big rake?
Well, smurf up the really big leaves, say!
Dopey Smurf is crazy!
All right! It's late! Let's get to bed! We'll continue tomorrow!
3
Peyo

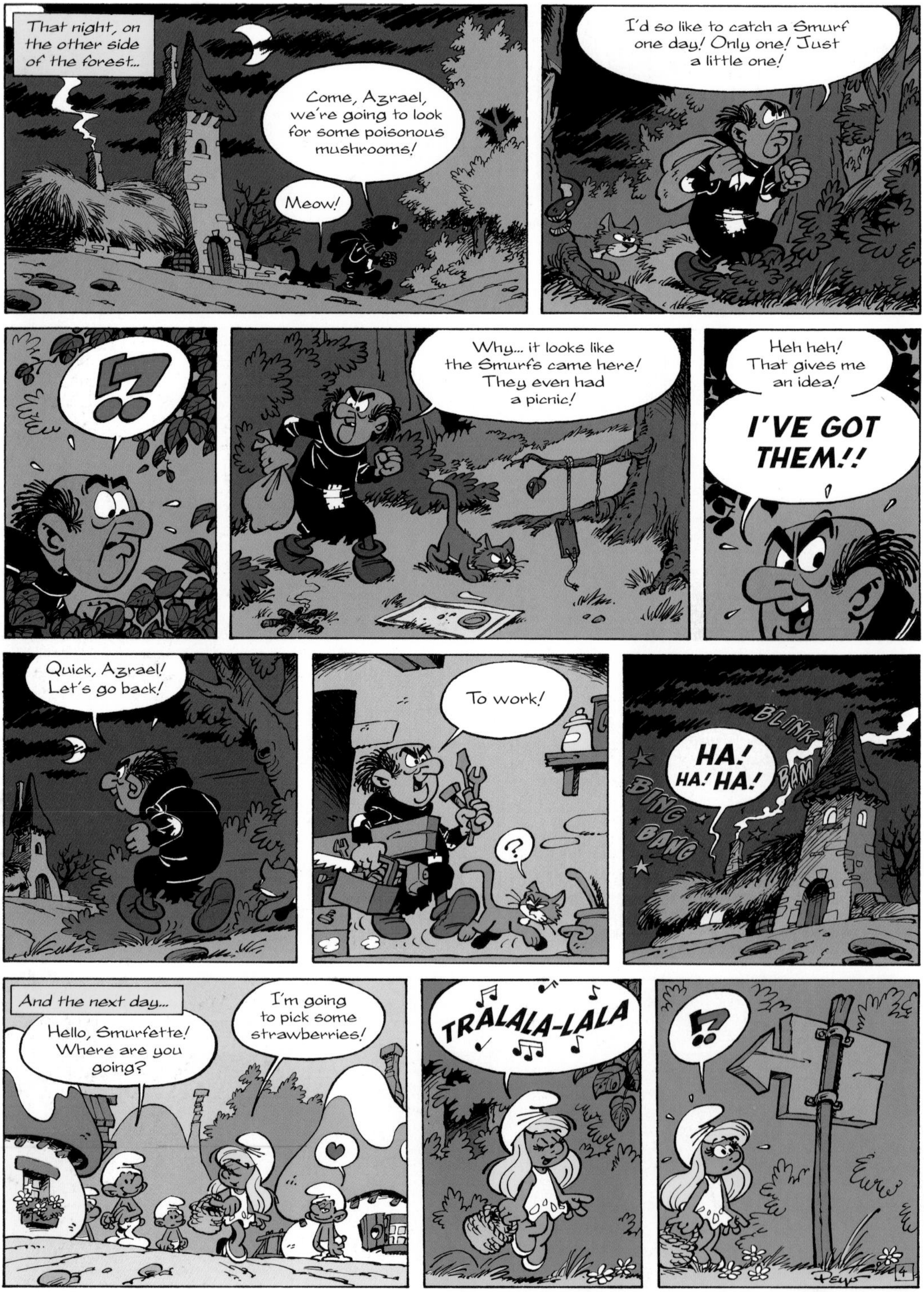
That night, on the other side of the forest...
Come, Azrael, we're going to look for some poisonous mushrooms!
Meow!
I'd so like to catch a Smurf one day! Only one! Just a little one!
Why... it looks like the Smurfs came here! They even had a picnic!
Heh heh! That gives me an idea!
I'VE GOT THEM!!
Quick, Azrael! Let's go back!
To work!
?
HA! HA! HA!
BLINK
BAM
BING
BANG
And the next day...
Hello, Smurfette! Where are you going?
I'm going to pick some strawberries!
TRALALA-LALA
4

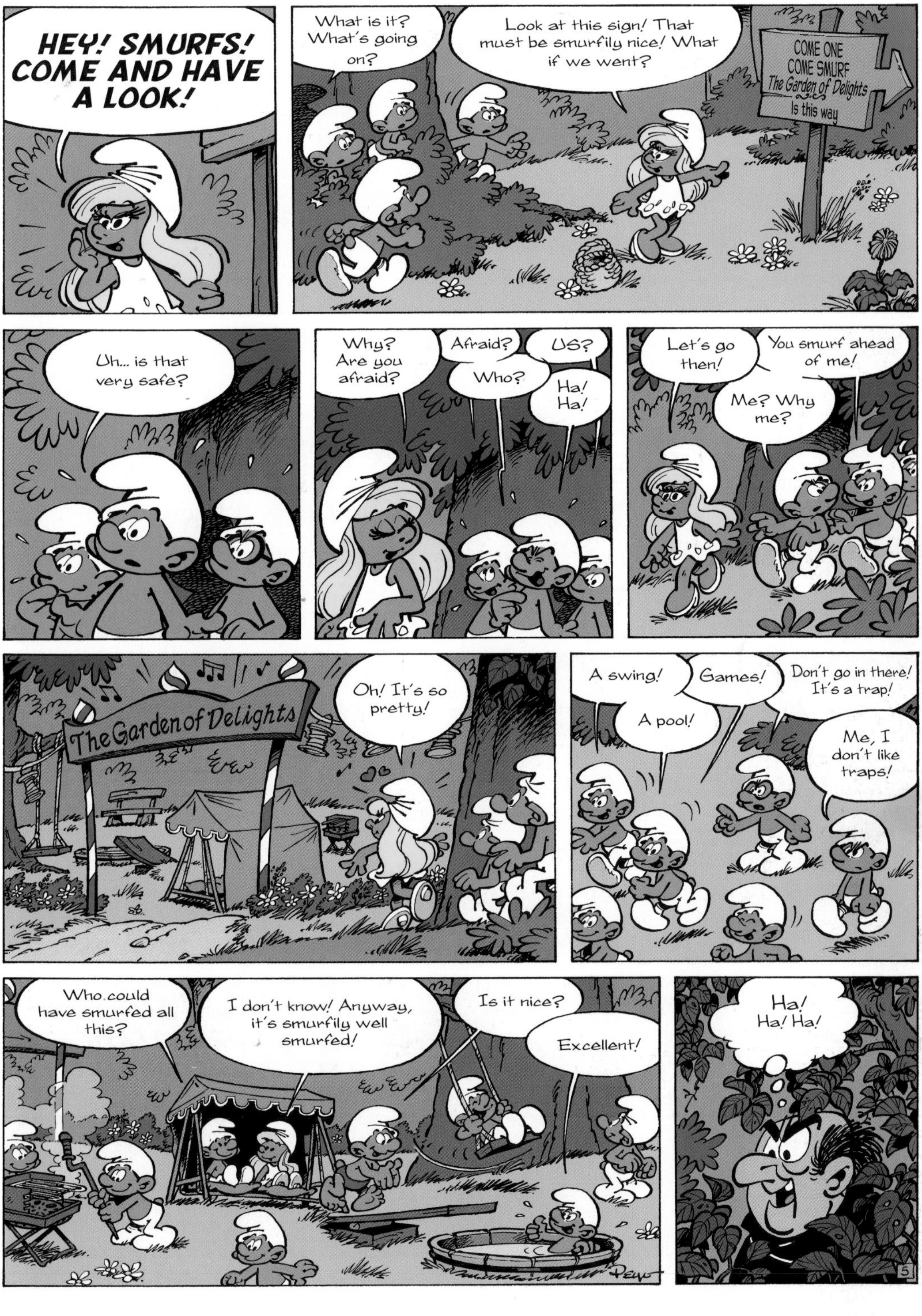
HEY! SMURFS! COME AND HAVE A LOOK!
What is it? What's going on?
Look at this sign! That must be smurfily nice! What if we went?
COME ONE COME SMURF The Garden of Delights Is this way
Uh... is that very safe?
Why? Are you afraid?
Afraid?
Who?
US?
Ha! Ha!
Let's go then!
You smurf ahead of me!
Me? Why me?
The Garden of Delights
Oh! It's so pretty!
A swing!
A pool!
Games!
Don't go in there! It's a trap!
Me, I don't like traps!
Who could have smurfed all this?
I don't know! Anyway, it's smurfily well smurfed!
Is it nice?
Excellent!
Ha! Ha! Ha!
5

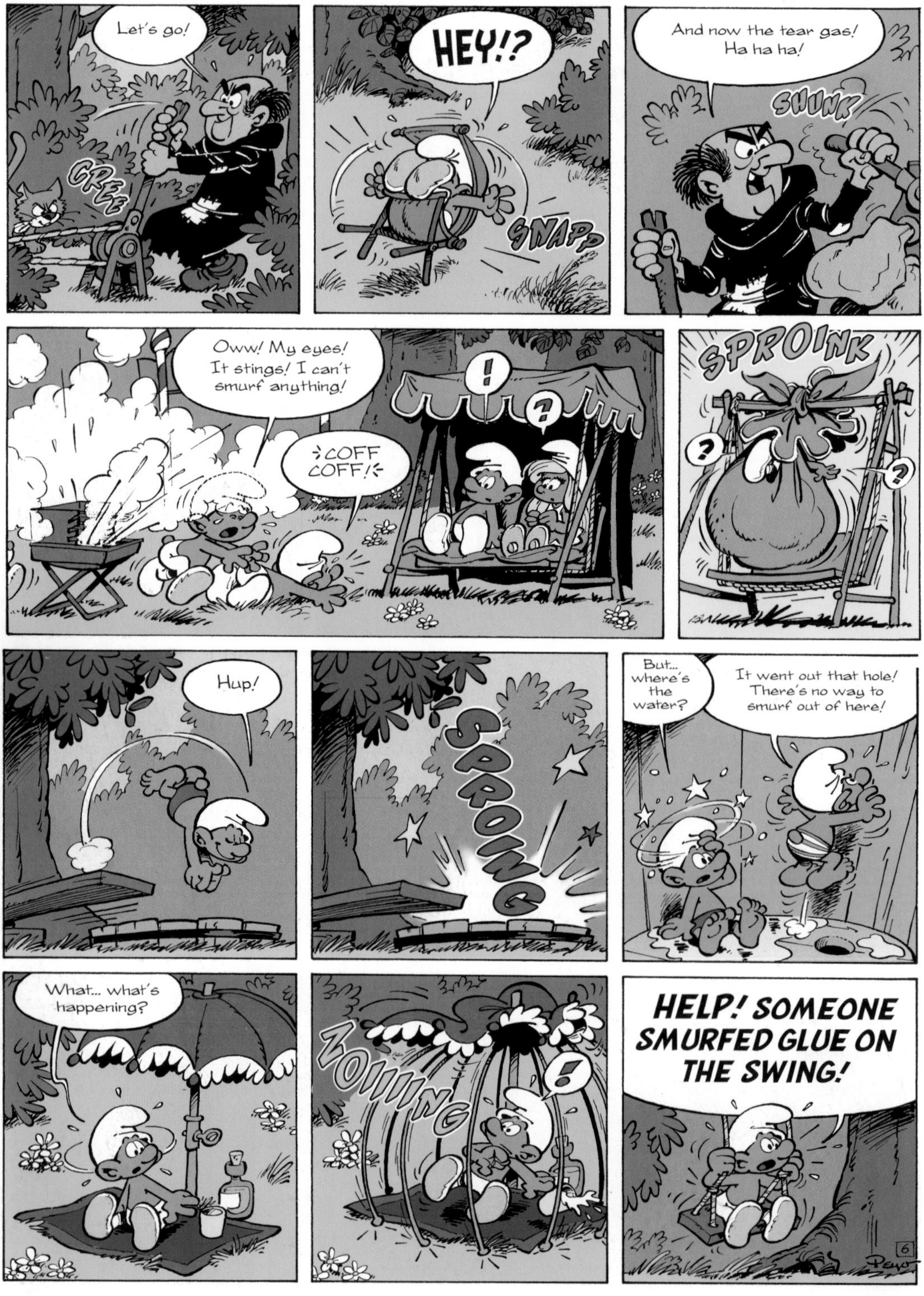
Let's go!
CREEE
HEY!?
SNAPP
And now the tear gas! Ha ha ha!
SHUNK
Oww! My eyes! It stings! I can't smurf anything!
COFF COFF!
!
?
SPROINK
?
?
Hup!
SPROING
But... where's the water?
It went out that hole! There's no way to smurf out of here!
What... what's happening?
ZOIIIING
!
HELP! SOMEONE SMURFED GLUE ON THE SWING!
6

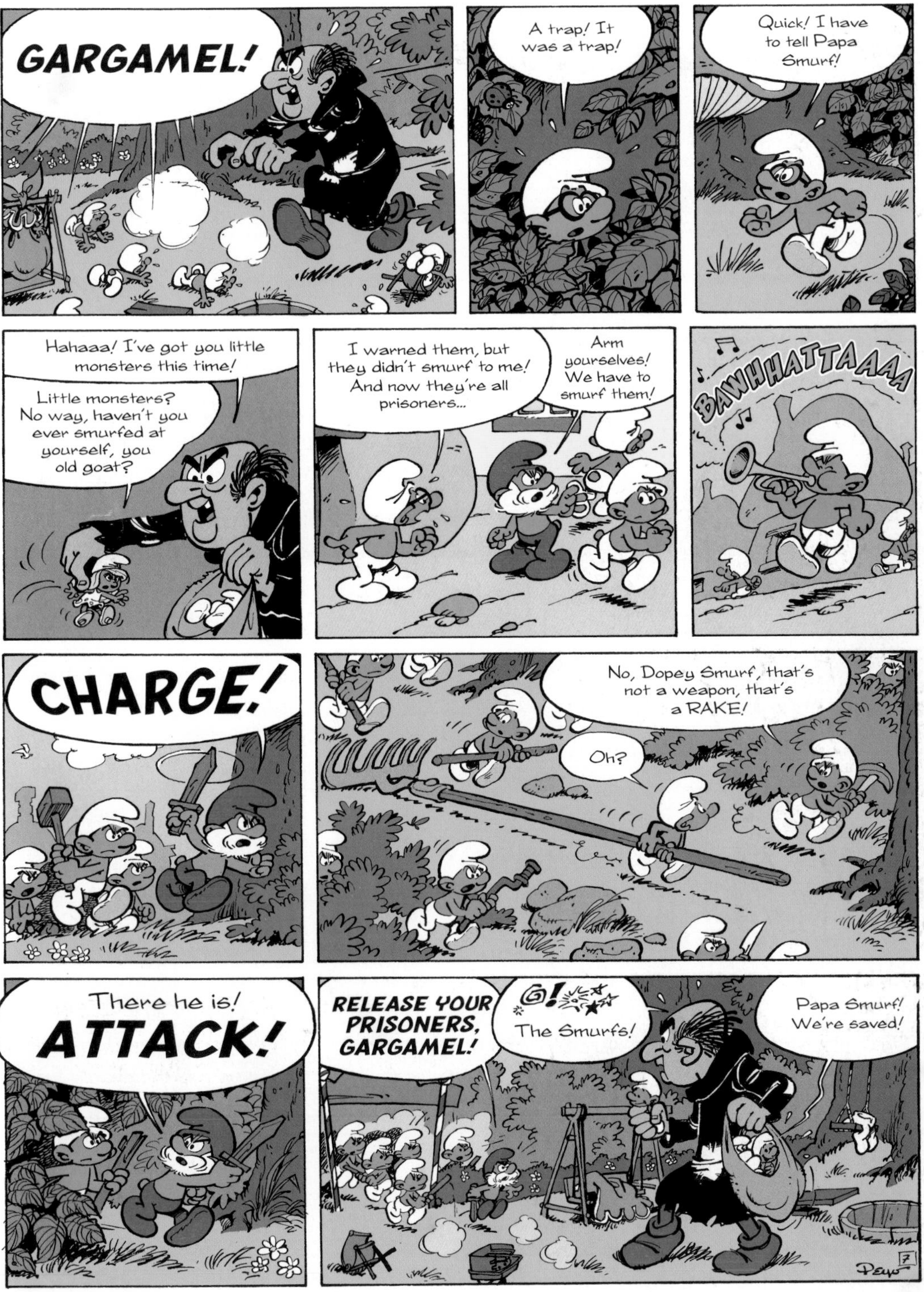
GARGAMEL!
A trap! It was a trap!
Quick! I have to tell Papa Smurf!
Hahaaa! I've got you little monsters this time!
Little monsters? No way, haven't you ever smurfed at yourself, you old goat?
I warned them, but they didn't smurf to me! And now they're all prisoners...
Arm yourselves! We have to smurf them!
BAWHHATTAAAA
CHARGE!
No, Dopey Smurf, that's not a weapon, that's a RAKE!
Oh?
There he is! ATTACK!
RELEASE YOUR PRISONERS, GARGAMEL!
The Smurfs!
Papa Smurf! We're saved!
7
Peyo

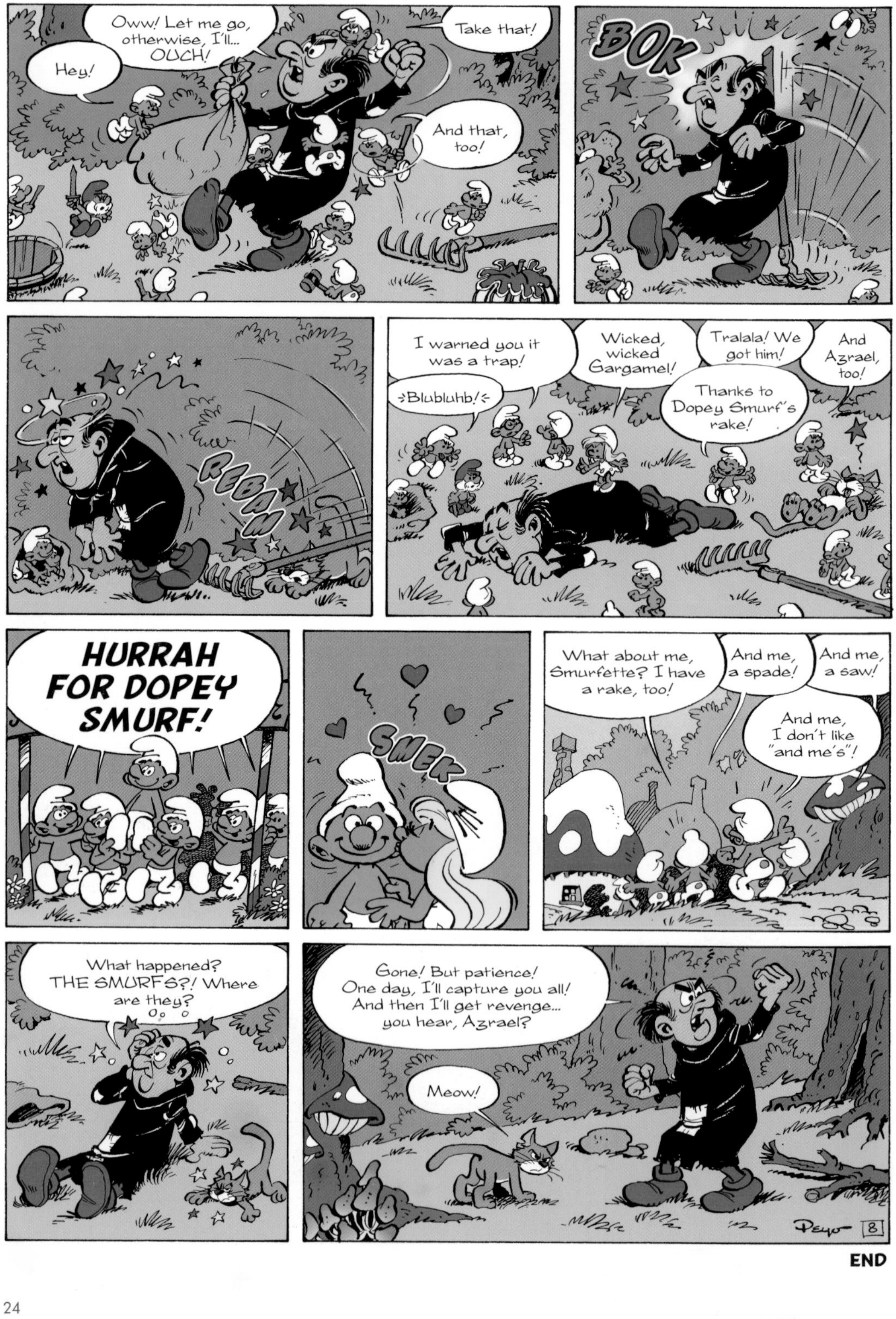
Hey!
Oww! Let me go, otherwise, I'll... OUCH!
Take that!
And that, too!
BOK
REBAM
I warned you it was a trap!
≻Blubluhb!≺
Wicked, wicked Gargamel!
Tralala! We got him!
And Azrael, too!
Thanks to Dopey Smurf's rake!
HURRAH FOR DOPEY SMURF!
SMEK
What about me, Smurfette? I have a rake, too!
And me, a spade!
And me, a saw!
And me, I don't like "and me's"!
What happened? THE SMURFS?! Where are they?
Gone! But patience! One day, I'll capture you all! And then I'll get revenge... you hear, Azrael?
Meow!
8

END

THE HANDY SMURF

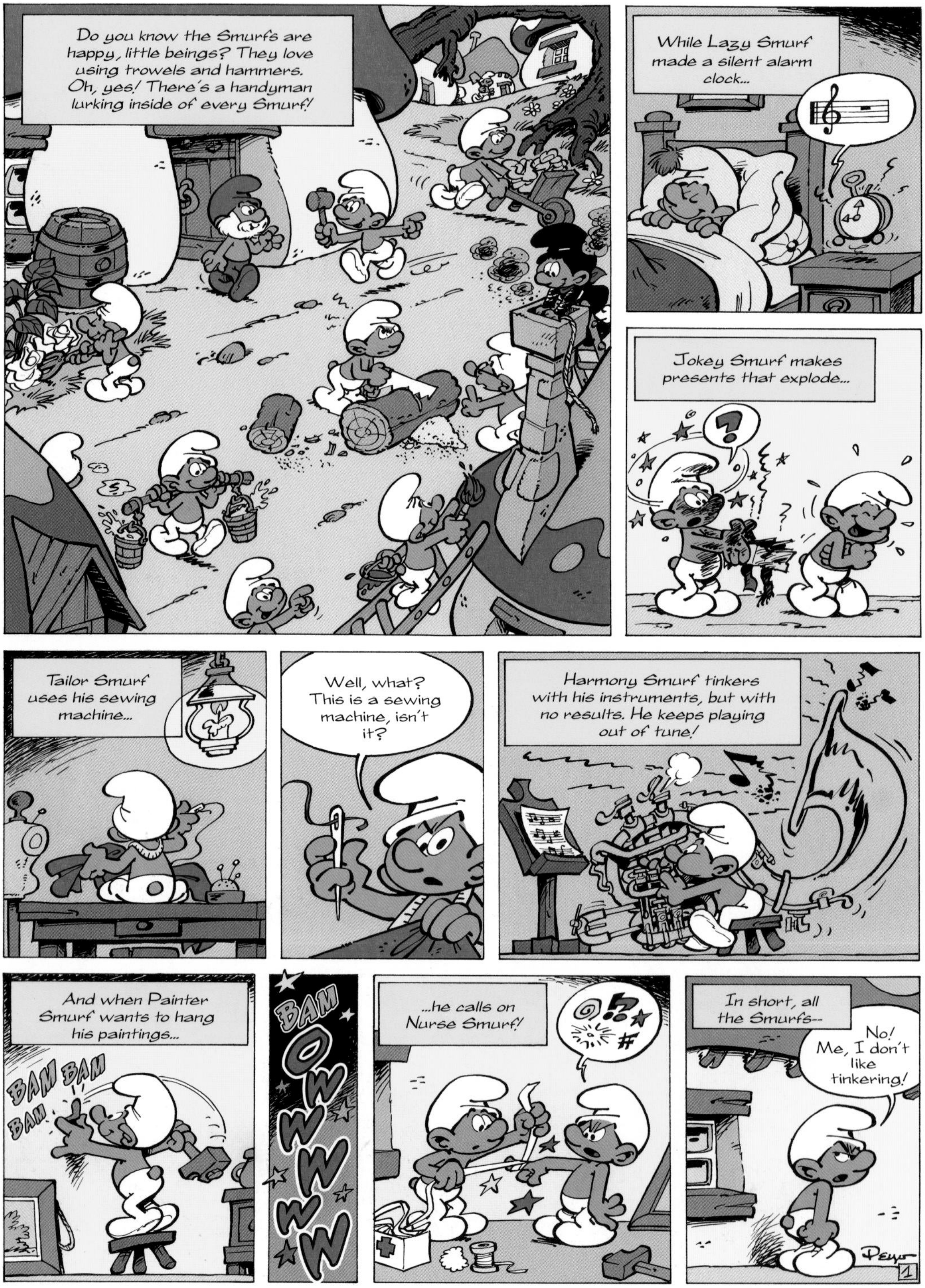
Do you know the Smurfs are happy, little beings? They love using trowels and hammers. Oh, yes! There's a handyman lurking inside of every Smurf!
While Lazy Smurf made a silent alarm clock...
Jokey Smurf makes presents that explode...
Tailor Smurf uses his sewing machine...
Well, what? This is a sewing machine, isn't it?
Harmony Smurf tinkers with his instruments, but with no results. He keeps playing out of tune!
And when Painter Smurf wants to hang his paintings...
BAM BAM
BAM
BAM
OWWWWWW
...he calls on Nurse Smurf!
In short, all the Smurfs--
No! Me, I don't like tinkering!
1

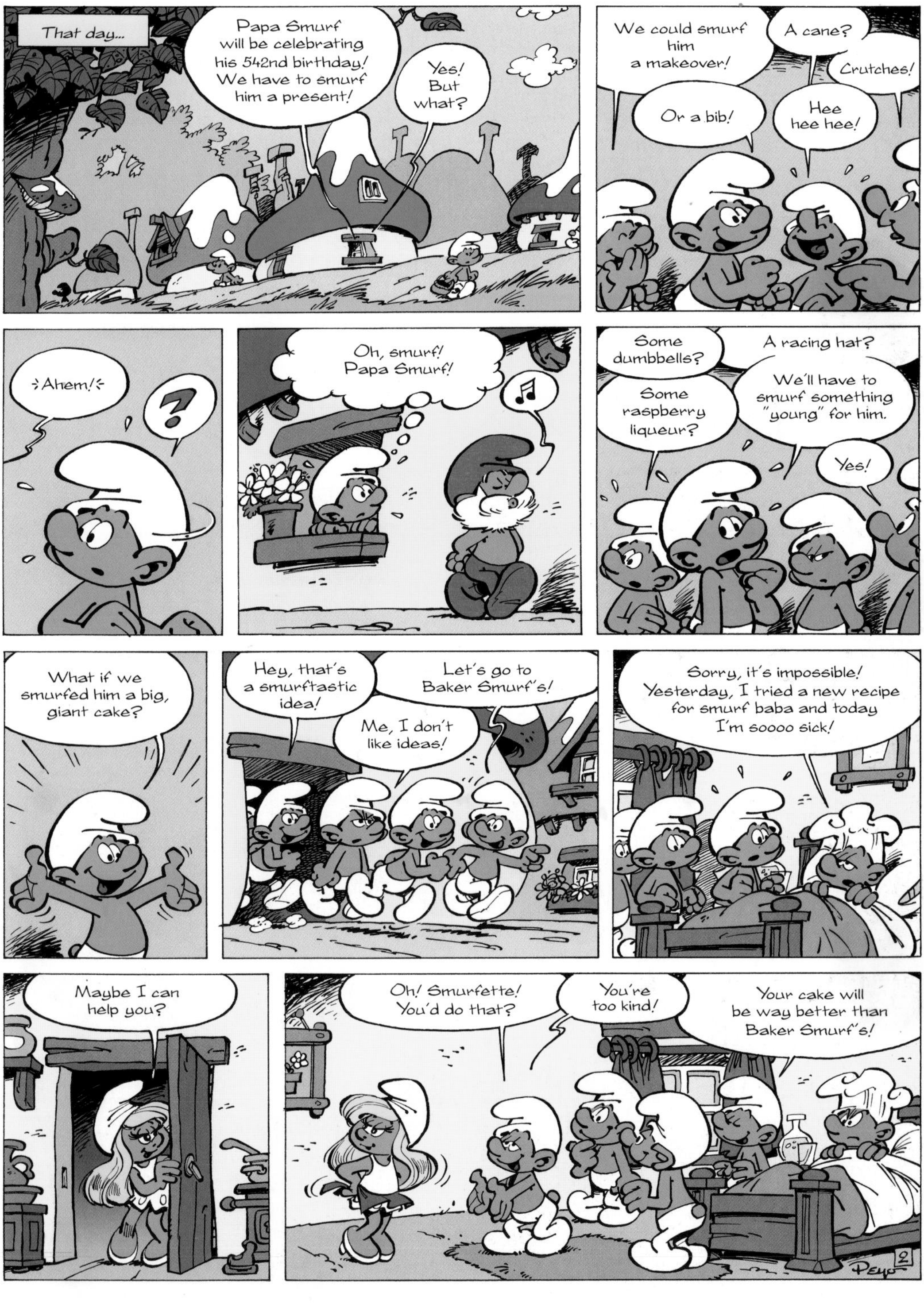

That day...
Papa Smurf will be celebrating his 542nd birthday! We have to smurf him a present!
Yes! But what?
We could smurf him a makeover!
A cane?
Crutches!
Or a bib!
Hee hee hee!
Ahem!
?
Oh, smurf! Papa Smurf!
Some dumbbells?
A racing hat?
Some raspberry liqueur?
We'll have to smurf something "young" for him.
Yes!
What if we smurfed him a big, giant cake?
Hey, that's a smurftastic idea!
Let's go to Baker Smurf's!
Me, I don't like ideas!
Sorry, it's impossible! Yesterday, I tried a new recipe for smurf baba and today I'm soooo sick!
Maybe I can help you?
Oh! Smurfette! You'd do that?
You're too kind!
Your cake will be way better than Baker Smurf's!
2
PEYO

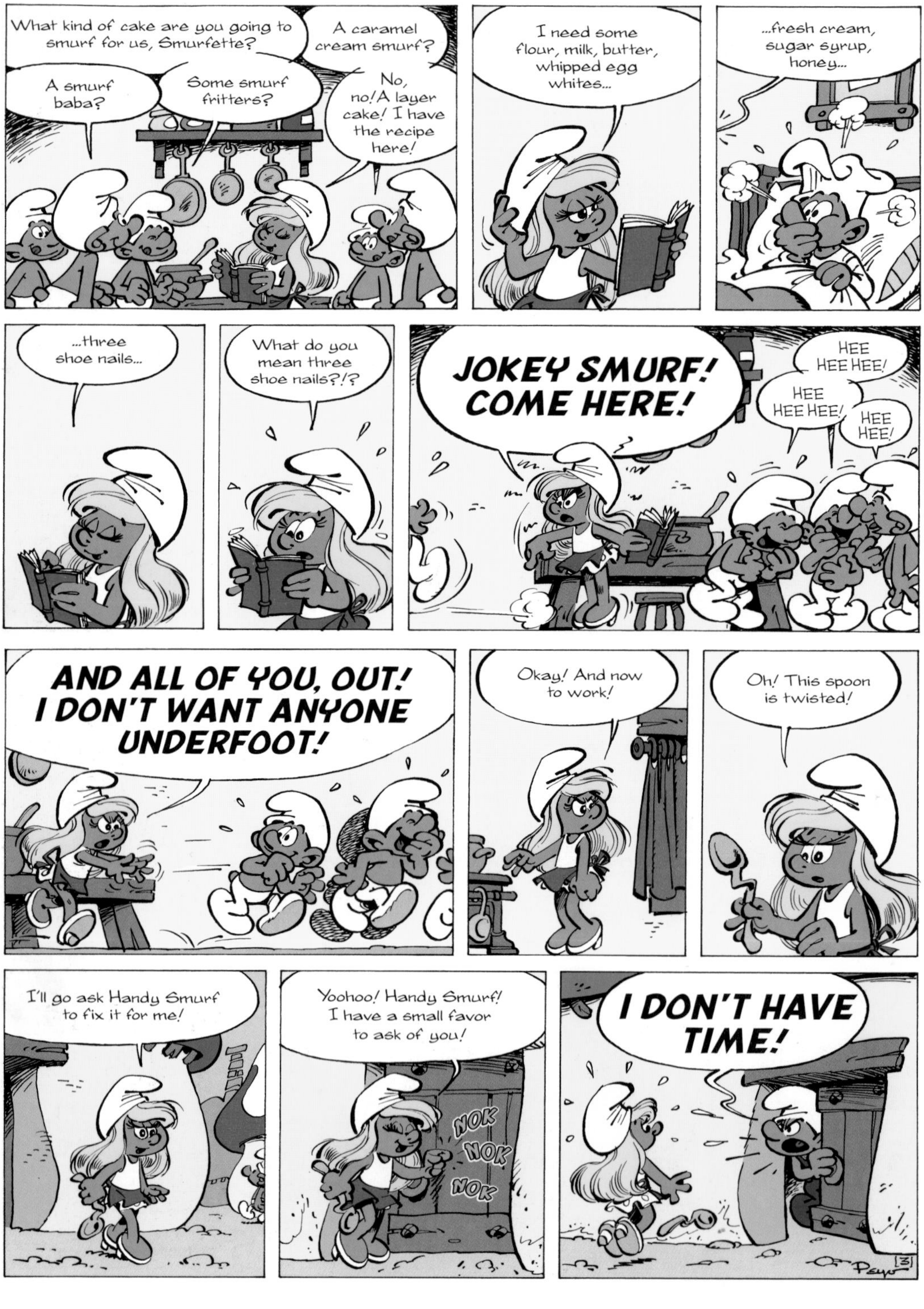
What kind of cake are you going to smurf for us, Smurfette?
A caramel cream smurf?
A smurf baba?
Some smurf fritters?
No, no! A layer cake! I have the recipe here!
I need some flour, milk, butter, whipped egg whites...
...fresh cream, sugar syrup, honey...
...three shoe nails...
What do you mean three shoe nails?!?
JOKEY SMURF! COME HERE!
HEE HEE HEE!
HEE HEE HEE!
HEE HEE!
AND ALL OF YOU, OUT! I DON'T WANT ANYONE UNDERFOOT!
Okay! And now to work!
Oh! This spoon is twisted!
I'll go ask Handy Smurf to fix it for me!
Yoohoo! Handy Smurf! I have a small favor to ask of you!
NOK
NOK
NOK
I DON'T HAVE TIME!
Peyo

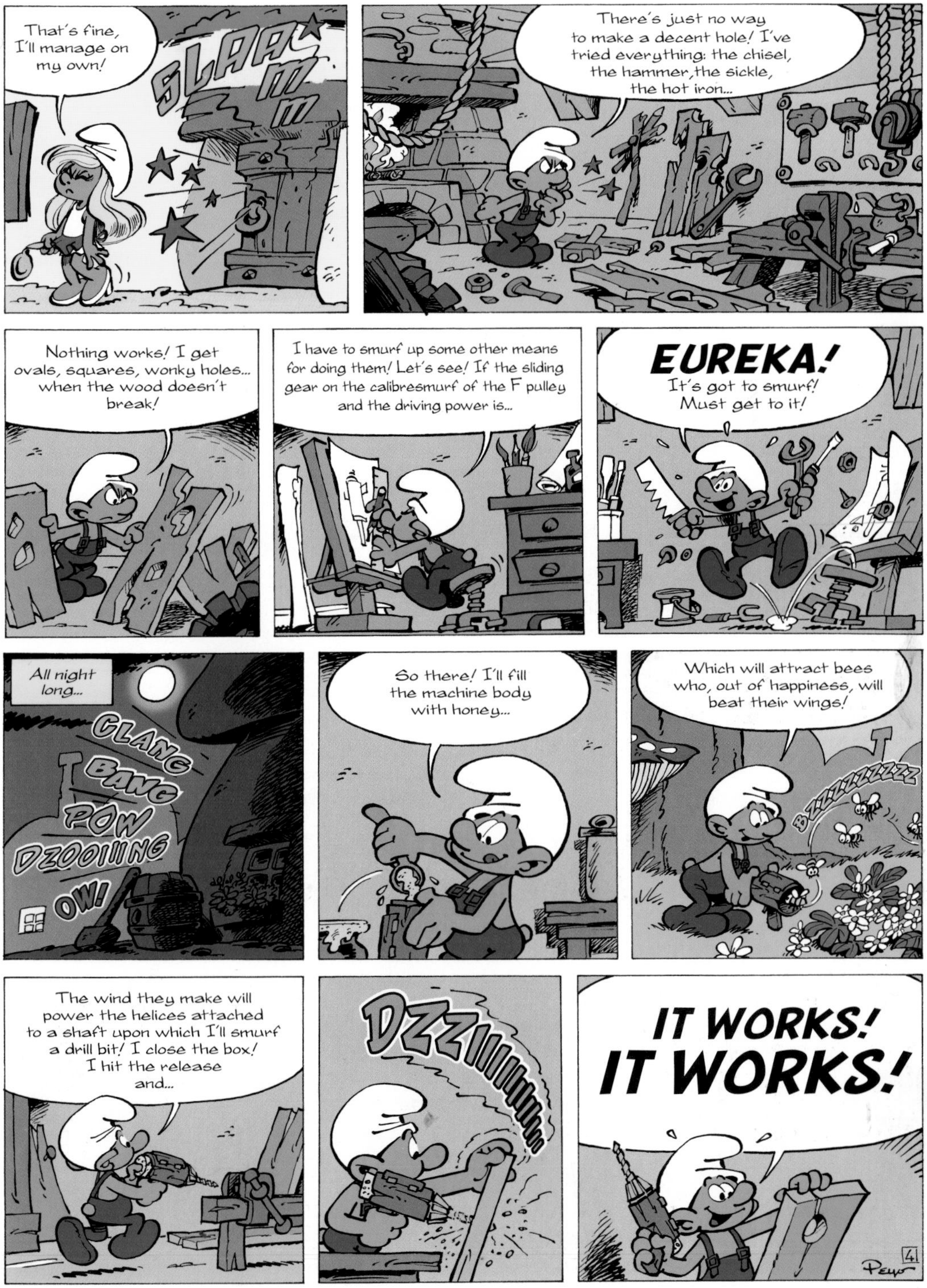
That's fine, I'll manage on my own!
SLAAMM
There's just no way to make a decent hole! I've tried everything: the chisel, the hammer, the sickle, the hot iron...
Nothing works! I get ovals, squares, wonky holes... when the wood doesn't break!
I have to smurf up some other means for doing them! Let's see! If the sliding gear on the calibresmurf of the F pulley and the driving power is...
EUREKA!
It's got to smurf! Must get to it!
All night long...
CLANG
BANG
POW
DZOOIIIING
OW!
So there! I'll fill the machine body with honey...
Which will attract bees who, out of happiness, will beat their wings!
BZZZZZZZZZZ
The wind they make will power the helices attached to a shaft upon which I'll smurf a drill bit! I close the box! I hit the release and...
DZZIIIIIIIIII
IT WORKS! IT WORKS!
41
Peyo

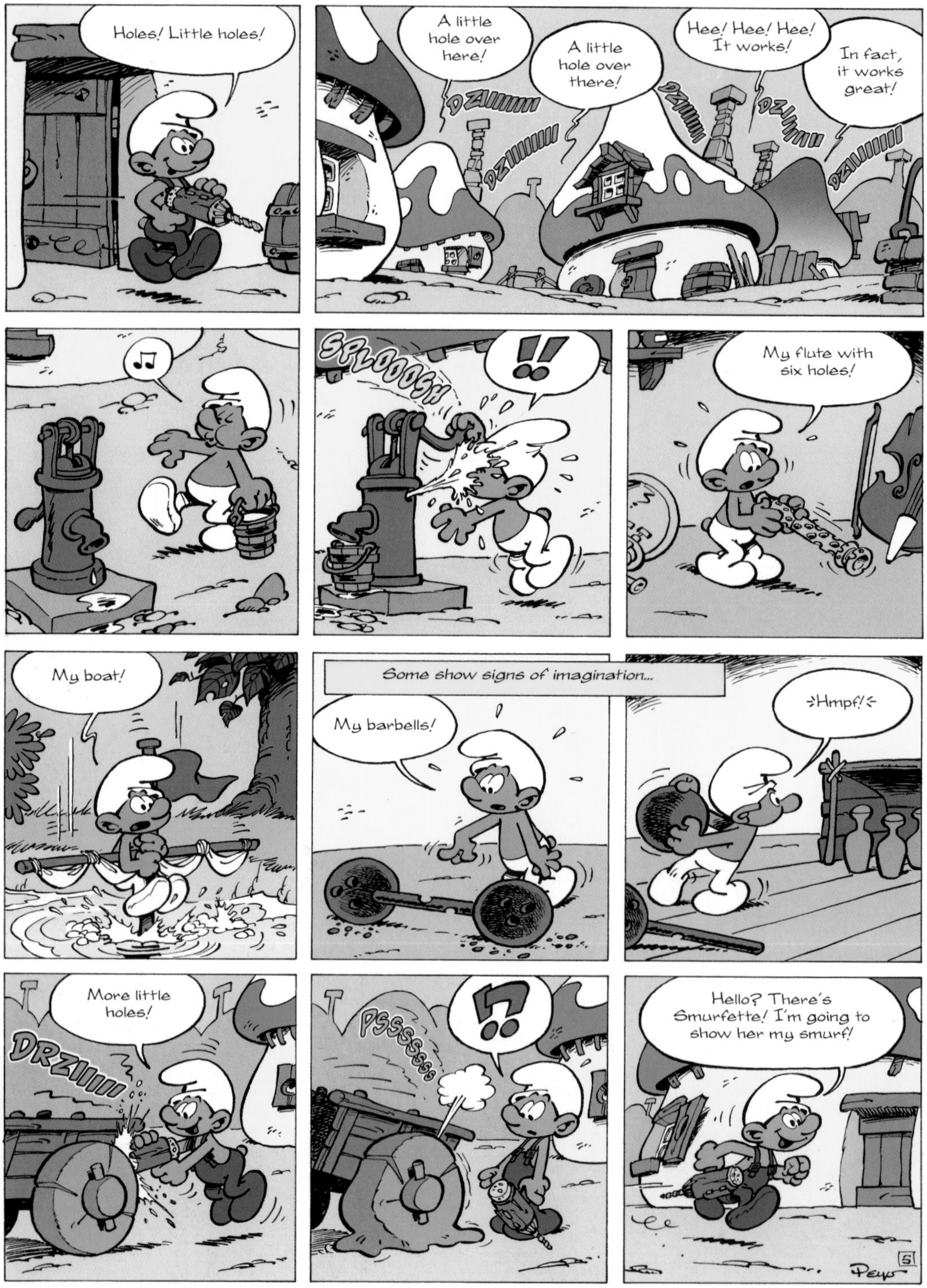
Holes! Little holes!
A little hole over here!
DZIIIIIII
A little hole over there!
DZIIIIIIII
Hee! Hee! Hee! It works!
DZIIIIIII
DZIIIIIIII
In fact, it works great!
DZIIIIIIII
♫
SPLOOOSH
!!
My flute with six holes!
My boat!
Some show signs of imagination...
My barbells!
Hmpf!
More little holes!
DRZIIIIII
PSSSSSSS
?!
Hello? There's Smurfette! I'm going to show her my smurf!
5
Peyo

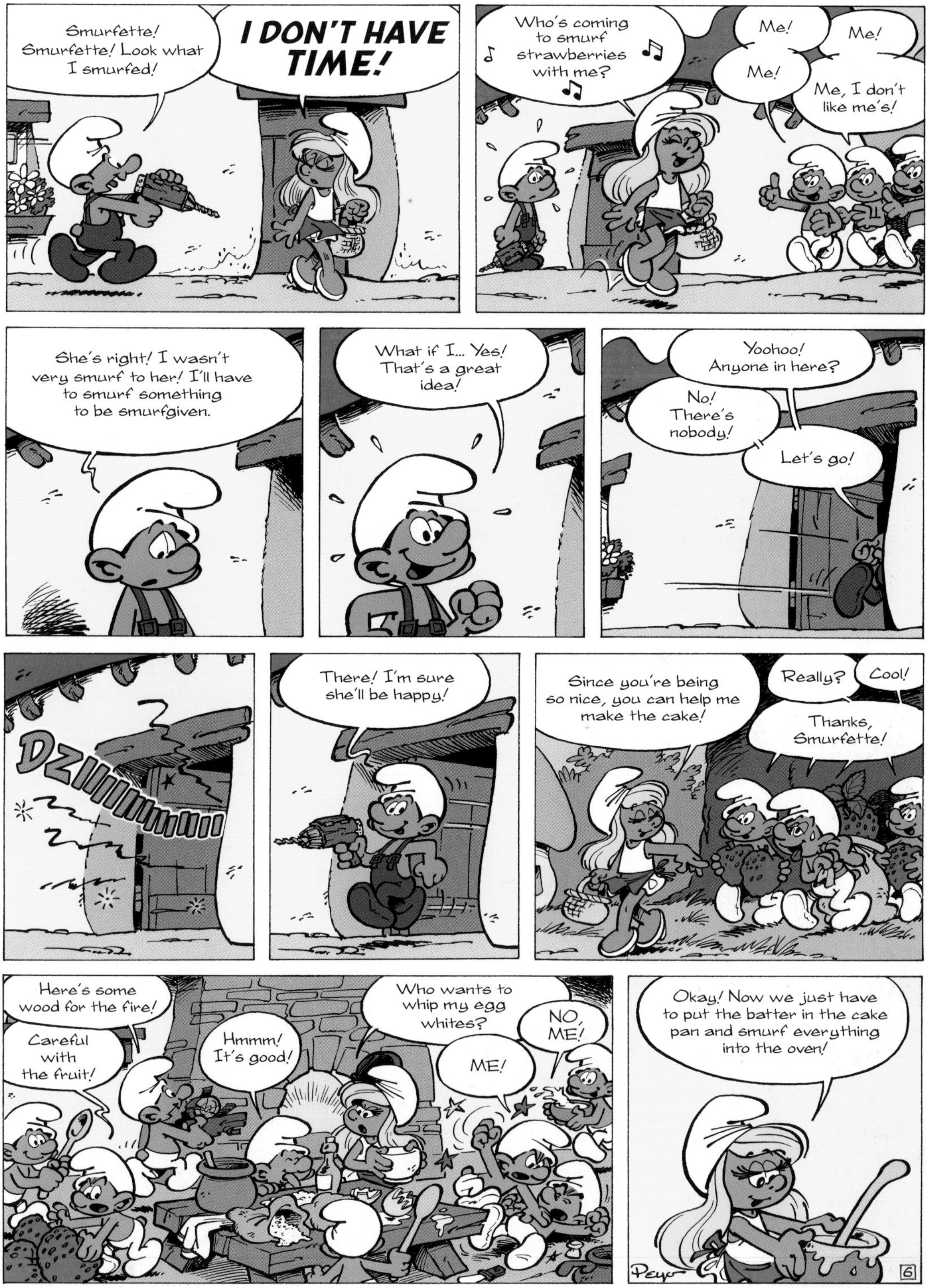
Smurfette! Smurfette! Look what I smurfed!
I DON'T HAVE TIME!
Who's coming to smurf strawberries with me?
Me!
Me!
Me!
Me, I don't like me's!
She's right! I wasn't very smurf to her! I'll have to smurf something to be smurfgiven.
What if I... Yes! That's a great idea!
Yoohoo! Anyone in here?
No! There's nobody!
Let's go!
DZIIIIIIIIIII
There! I'm sure she'll be happy!
Since you're being so nice, you can help me make the cake!
Really?
Cool!
Thanks, Smurfette!
Here's some wood for the fire!
Careful with the fruit!
Hmmm! It's good!
Who wants to whip my egg whites?
ME!
NO, ME!
Okay! Now we just have to put the batter in the cake pan and smurf everything into the oven!
Peyo
6

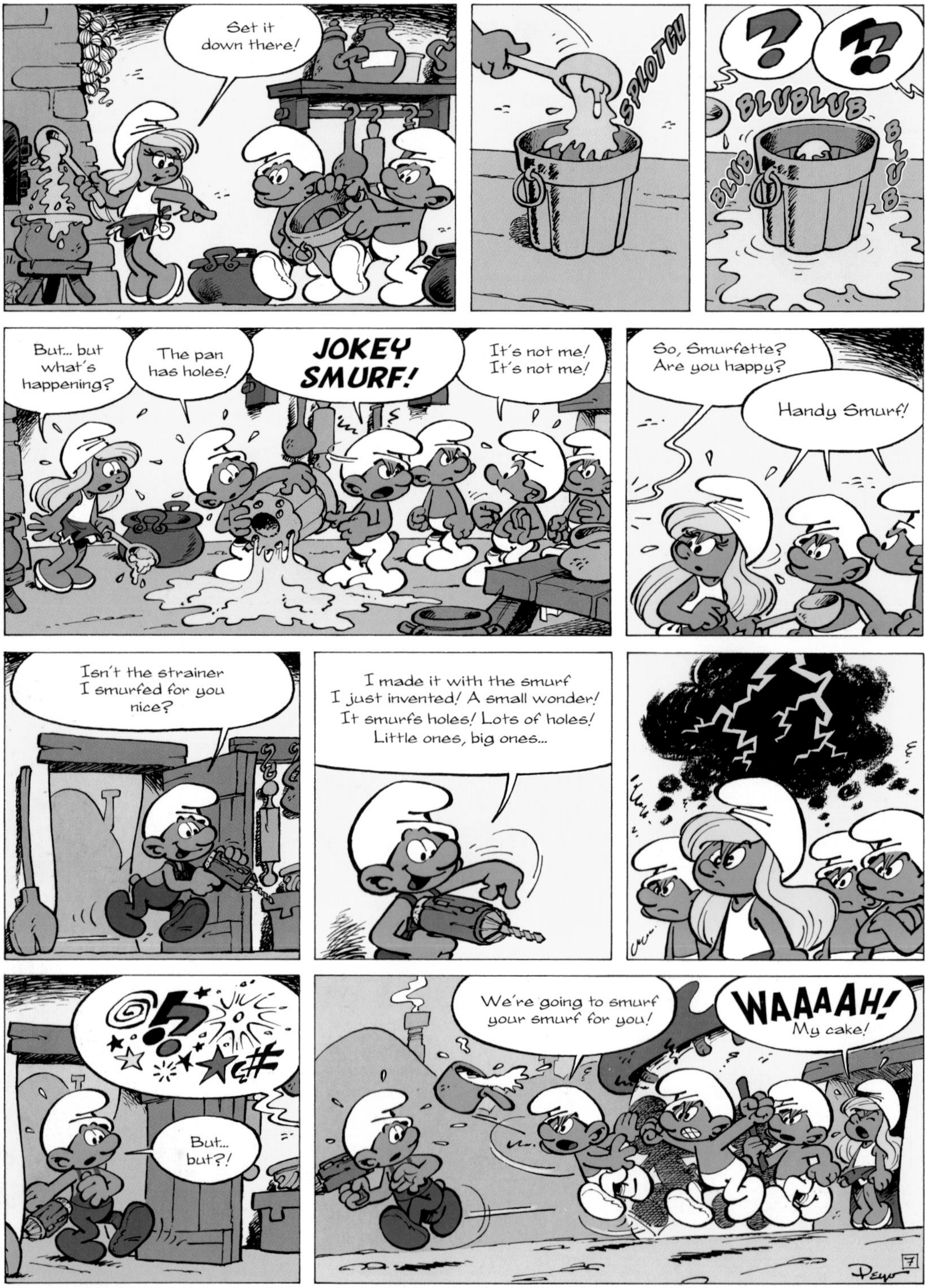
Set it down there!
SPLOTCH
BLUBLUB
BLUB
BLUB
But... but what's happening?
The pan has holes!
JOKEY SMURF!
It's not me! It's not me!
So, Smurfette? Are you happy?
Handy Smurf!
Isn't the strainer I smurfed for you nice?
I made it with the smurf I just invented! A small wonder! It smurfs holes! Lots of holes! Little ones, big ones...
But... but?!
We're going to smurf your smurf for you!
WAAAAH! My cake!
7
Peyo

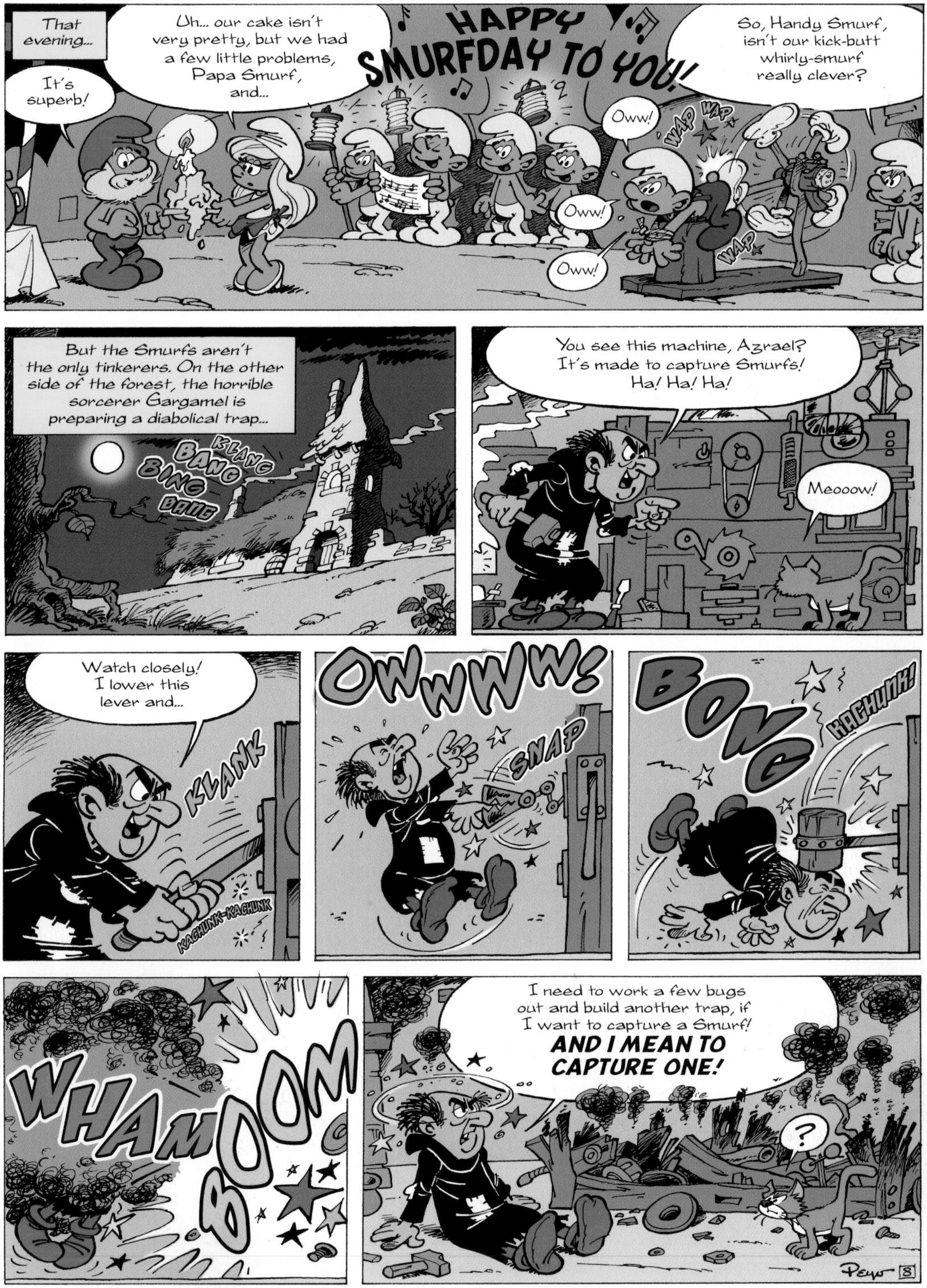
That evening...
It's superb!
Uh... our cake isn't very pretty, but we had a few little problems, Papa Smurf, and...
HAPPY SMURFDAY TO YOU!
So, Handy Smurf, isn't our kick-butt whirly-smurf really clever?
Oww!
WAP WAP
Oww!
Oww!
WAP
But the Smurfs aren't the only tinkerers. On the other side of the forest, the horrible sorcerer Gargamel is preparing a diabolical trap...
KLANG BANG BING BANG
You see this machine, Azrael? It's made to capture Smurfs! Ha! Ha! Ha!
Meooow!
Watch closely! I lower this lever and...
KLANK
KACHUNK-KACHUNK
OWWWW!
SNAP
BONG
KACHUNK!
WHAMBOOM
I need to work a few bugs out and build another trap, if I want to capture a Smurf!
AND I MEAN TO CAPTURE ONE!
?
Peyo 8

THE END

More ROMEOS AND SMURFETTE

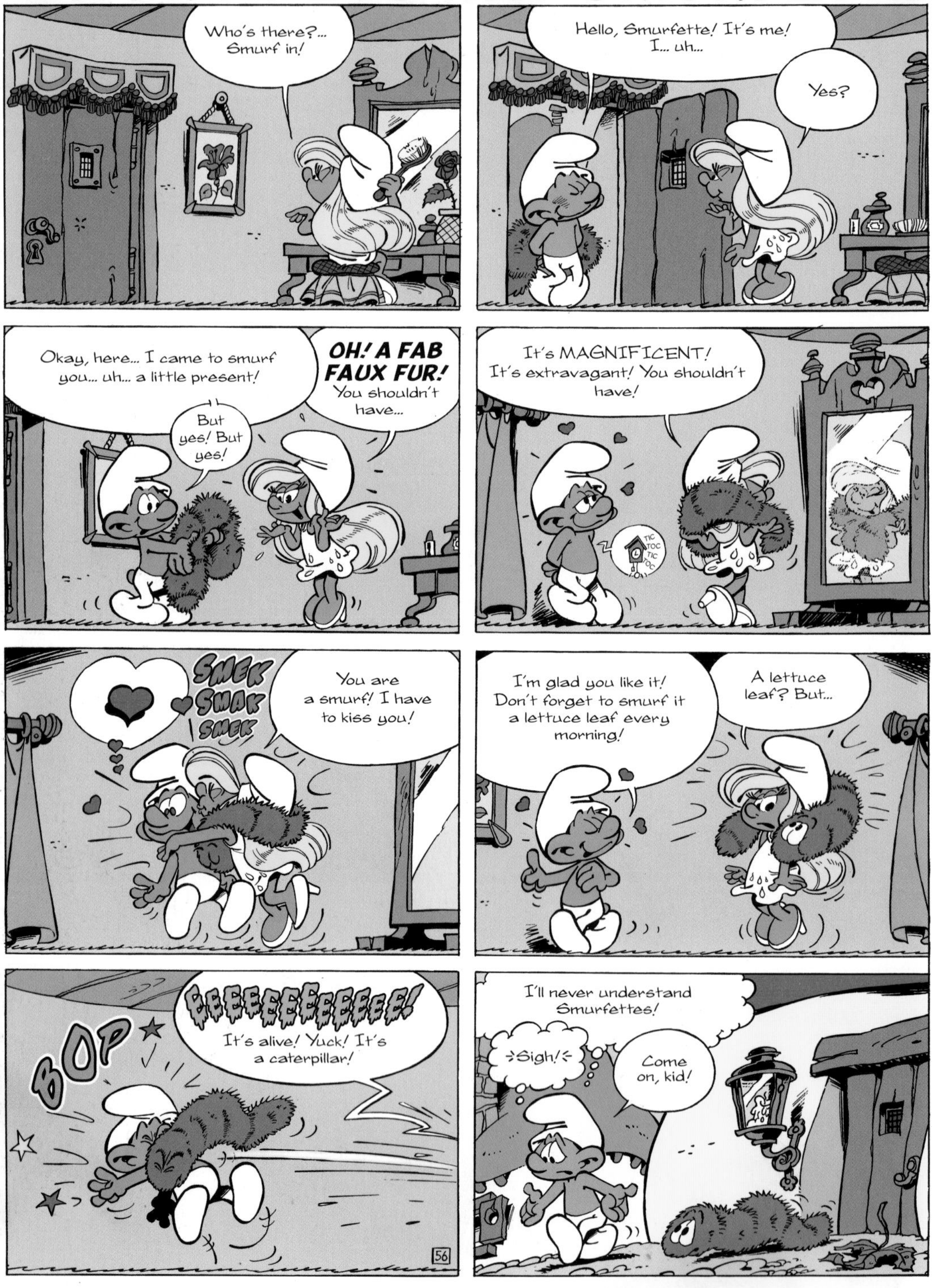

Who's there?... Smurf in!
Hello, Smurfette! It's me! I... uh...
Yes?
Okay, here... I came to smurf you... uh... a little present!
But yes! But yes!
OH! A FAB FAUX FUR! You shouldn't have...
It's MAGNIFICENT! It's extravagant! You shouldn't have!
TIC TOC TIC TOC
SMEK SMAK SMEK
You are a smurf! I have to kiss you!
I'm glad you like it! Don't forget to smurf it a lettuce leaf every morning!
A lettuce leaf? But...
BOP
EEEEEEEEEEEE!
It's alive! Yuck! It's a caterpillar!
56
I'll never understand Smurfettes!
Sigh!
Come on, kid!

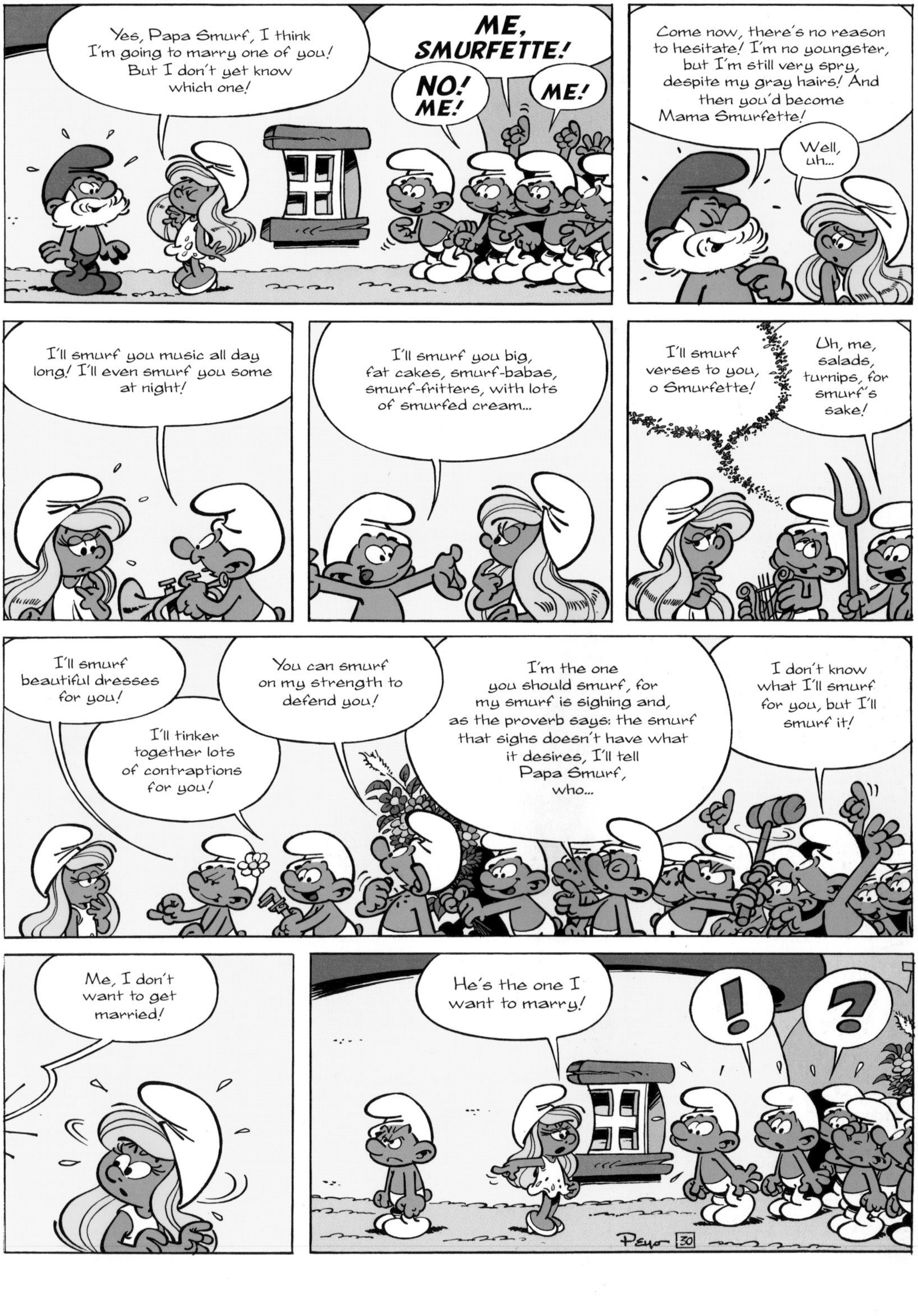
Yes, Papa Smurf, I think I'm going to marry one of you! But I don't yet know which one!
ME, SMURFETTE!
NO! ME!
ME!
Come now, there's no reason to hesitate! I'm no youngster, but I'm still very spry, despite my gray hairs! And then you'd become Mama Smurfette!
Well, uh...
I'll smurf you music all day long! I'll even smurf you some at night!
I'll smurf you big, fat cakes, smurf-babas, smurf-fritters, with lots of smurfed cream...
I'll smurf verses to you, o Smurfette!
Uh, me, salads, turnips, for smurf's sake!
I'll smurf beautiful dresses for you!
I'll tinker together lots of contraptions for you!
You can smurf on my strength to defend you!
I'm the one you should smurf, for my smurf is sighing and, as the proverb says: the smurf that sighs doesn't have what it desires, I'll tell Papa Smurf, who...
I don't know what I'll smurf for you, but I'll smurf it!
Me, I don't want to get married!
He's the one I want to marry!
!
?
Peyo 30

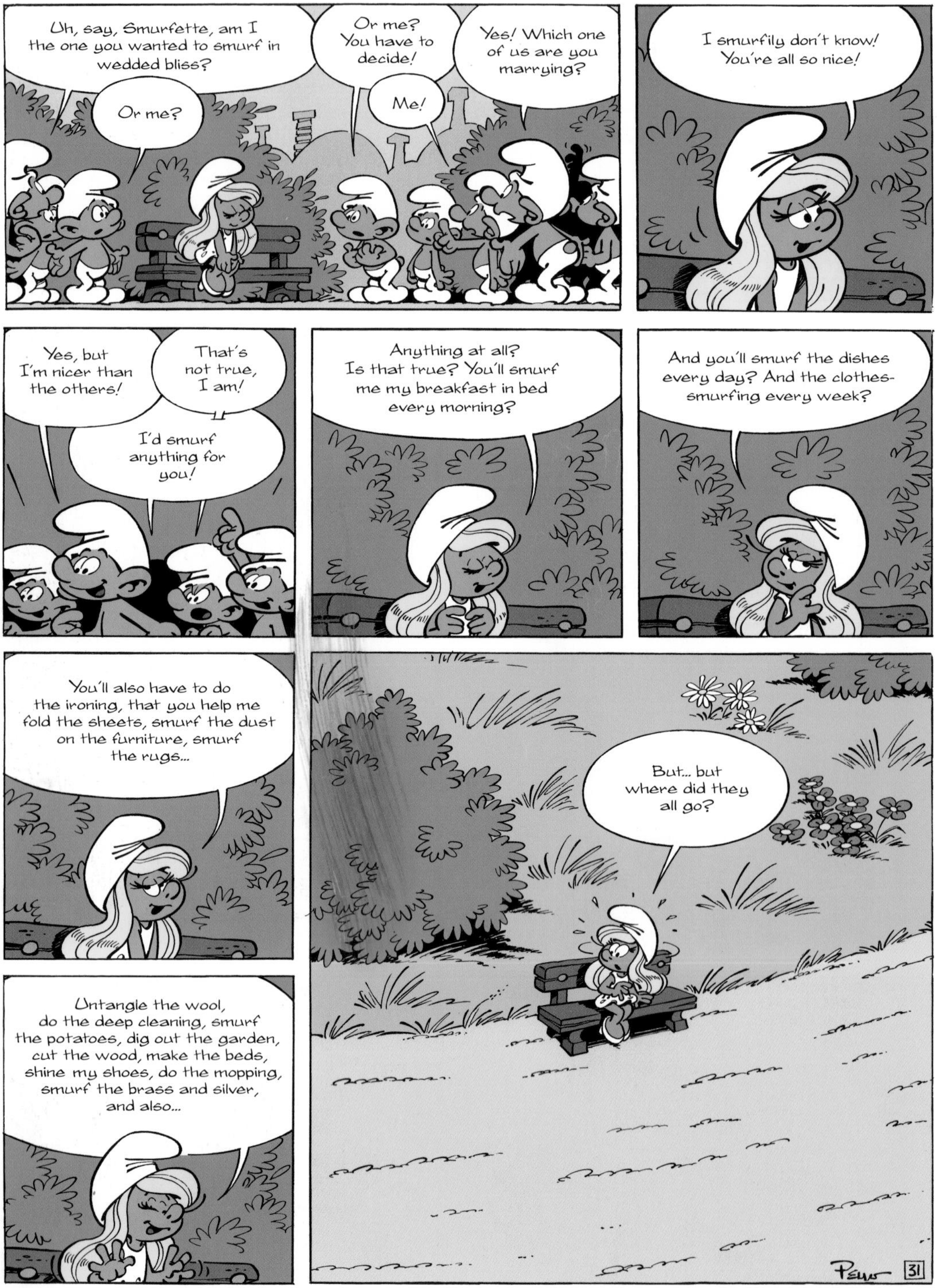

Uh, say, Smurfette, am I the one you wanted to smurf in wedded bliss?
Or me?
Or me? You have to decide!
Me!
Yes! Which one of us are you marrying?
I smurfily don't know! You're all so nice!
Yes, but I'm nicer than the others!
That's not true, I am!
I'd smurf anything for you!
Anything at all? Is that true? You'll smurf me my breakfast in bed every morning?
And you'll smurf the dishes every day? And the clothes-smurfing every week?
You'll also have to do the ironing, that you help me fold the sheets, smurf the dust on the furniture, smurf the rugs...
Untangle the wool, do the deep cleaning, smurf the potatoes, dig out the garden, cut the wood, make the beds, shine my shoes, do the mopping, smurf the brass and silver, and also...
But... but where did they all go?

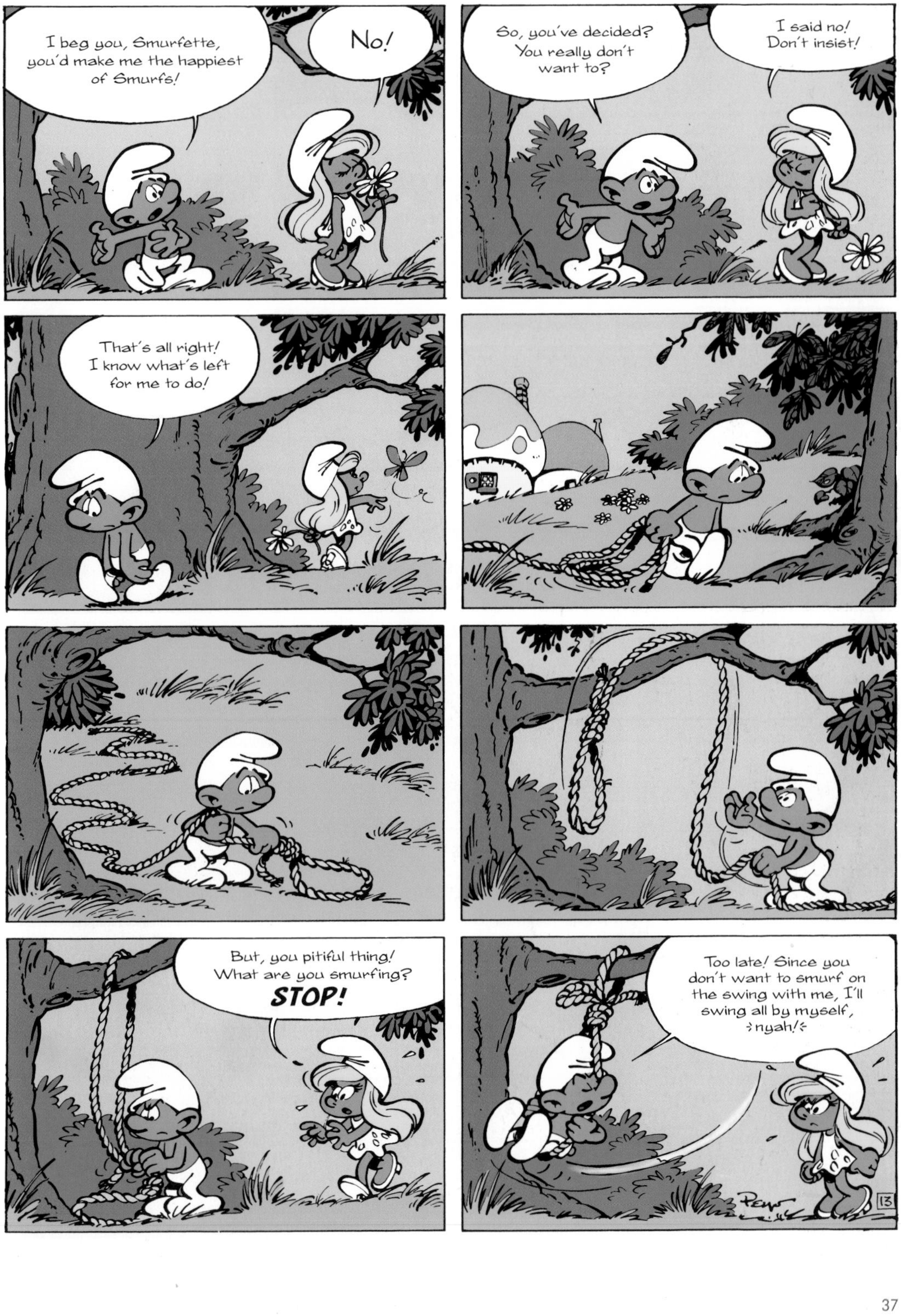

I beg you, Smurfette, you'd make me the happiest of Smurfs!
No!
So, you've decided? You really don't want to?
I said no! Don't insist!
That's all right! I know what's left for me to do!
But, you pitiful thing! What are you smurfing? **STOP!**
Too late! Since you don't want to smurf on the swing with me, I'll swing all by myself, nyah!

HALLOWEEN

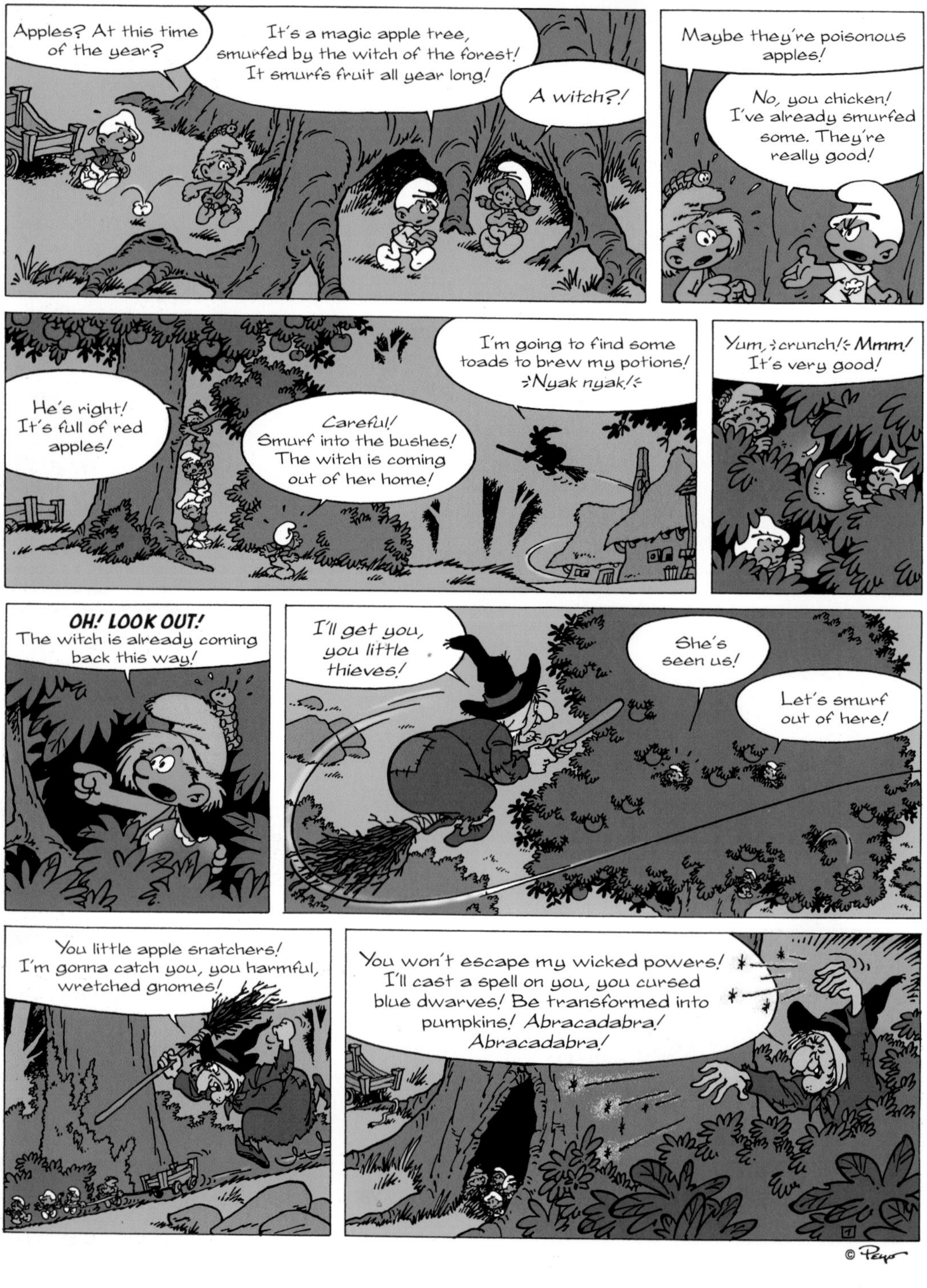

Apples? At this time of the year?
It's a magic apple tree, smurfed by the witch of the forest! It smurfs fruit all year long!
A witch?!
Maybe they're poisonous apples!
No, you chicken! I've already smurfed some. They're really good!
He's right! It's full of red apples!
I'm going to find some toads to brew my potions! Nyak nyak!
Careful! Smurf into the bushes! The witch is coming out of her home!
Yum, crunch! Mmm! It's very good!
OH! LOOK OUT! The witch is already coming back this way!
I'll get you, you little thieves!
She's seen us!
Let's smurf out of here!
You little apple snatchers! I'm gonna catch you, you harmful, wretched gnomes!
You won't escape my wicked powers! I'll cast a spell on you, you cursed blue dwarves! Be transformed into pumpkins! Abracadabra! Abracadabra!

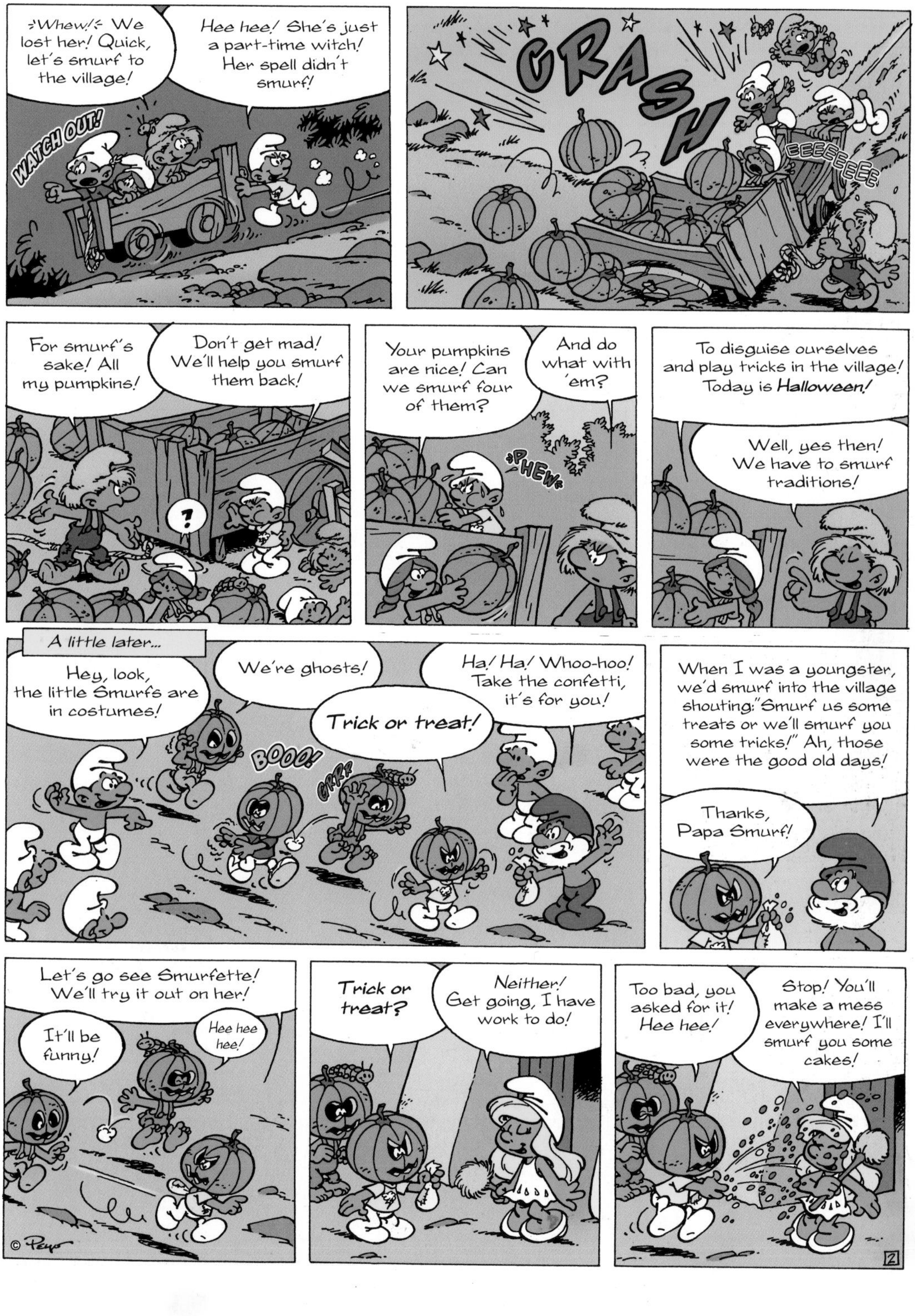

-Whew!- We lost her! Quick, let's smurf to the village!
Hee hee! She's just a part-time witch! Her spell didn't smurf!
WATCH OUT!
CRASH
EEEEEEEE
For smurf's sake! All my pumpkins!
Don't get mad! We'll help you smurf them back!
?
Your pumpkins are nice! Can we smurf four of them?
And do what with 'em?
PHEW
To disguise ourselves and play tricks in the village! Today is Halloween!
Well, yes then! We have to smurf traditions!
A little later...
Hey, look, the little Smurfs are in costumes!
We're ghosts!
Ha! Ha! Whoo-hoo! Take the confetti, it's for you!
Trick or treat!
BOOO!
GRRR
When I was a youngster, we'd smurf into the village shouting: "Smurf us some treats or we'll smurf you some tricks!" Ah, those were the good old days!
Thanks, Papa Smurf!
Let's go see Smurfette! We'll try it out on her!
It'll be funny!
Hee hee hee!
Trick or treat?
Neither! Get going, I have work to do!
Too bad, you asked for it! Hee hee!
Stop! You'll make a mess everywhere! I'll smurf you some cakes!
2

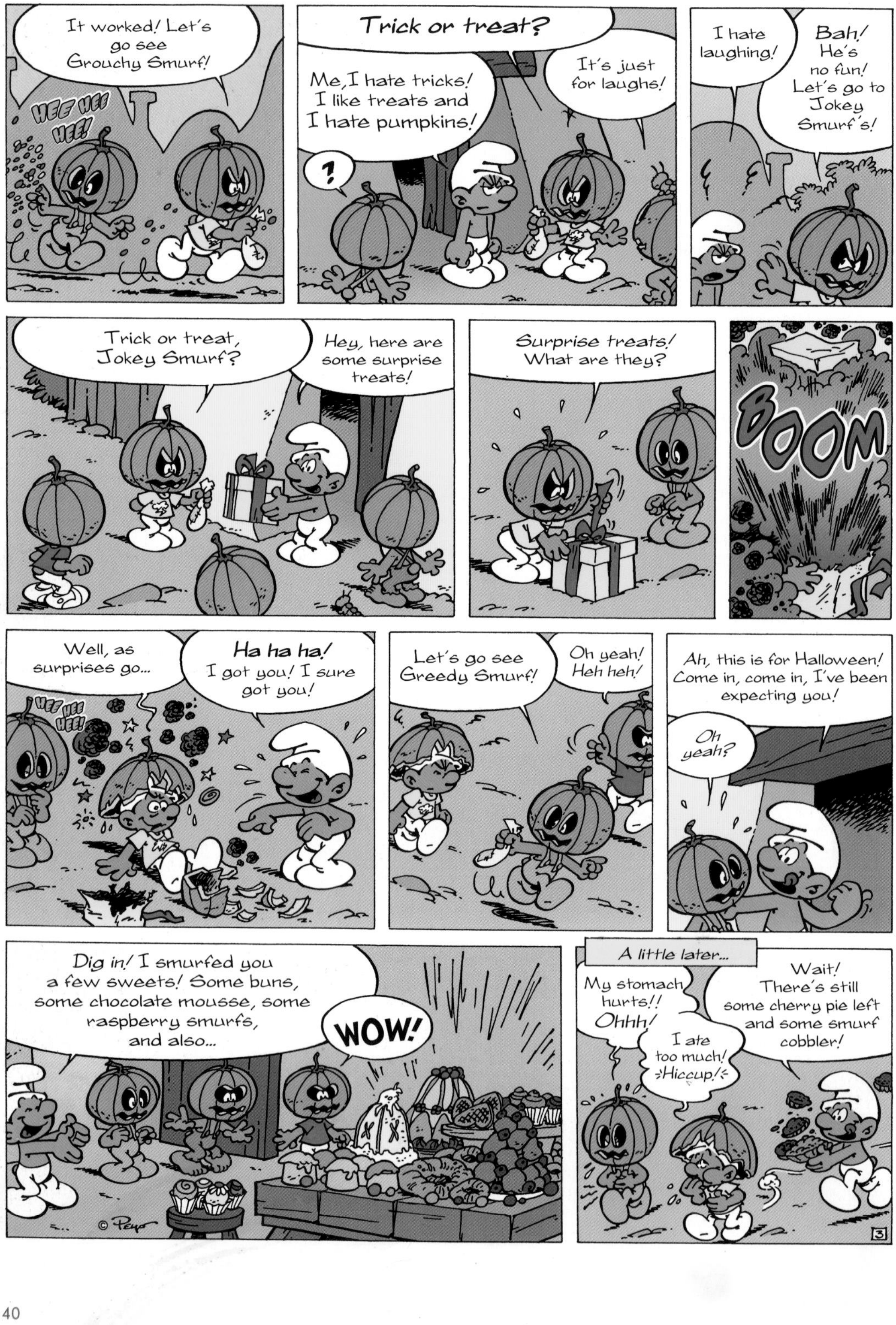

It worked! Let's go see Grouchy Smurf!
HEE HEE HEE!
Trick or treat?
Me, I hate tricks! I like treats and I hate pumpkins!
?
It's just for laughs!
I hate laughing!
Bah! He's no fun! Let's go to Jokey Smurf's!
Trick or treat, Jokey Smurf?
Hey, here are some surprise treats!
Surprise treats! What are they?
BOOM
Well, as surprises go...
HEE HEE HEE!
Ha ha ha! I got you! I sure got you!
Let's go see Greedy Smurf!
Oh yeah! Heh heh!
Ah, this is for Halloween! Come in, come in, I've been expecting you!
Oh yeah?
Dig in! I smurfed you a few sweets! Some buns, some chocolate mousse, some raspberry smurfs, and also...
WOW!
© Peyo
A little later...
My stomach hurts!! Ohhh!
I ate too much! Hiccup!
Wait! There's still some cherry pie left and some smurf cobbler!
3

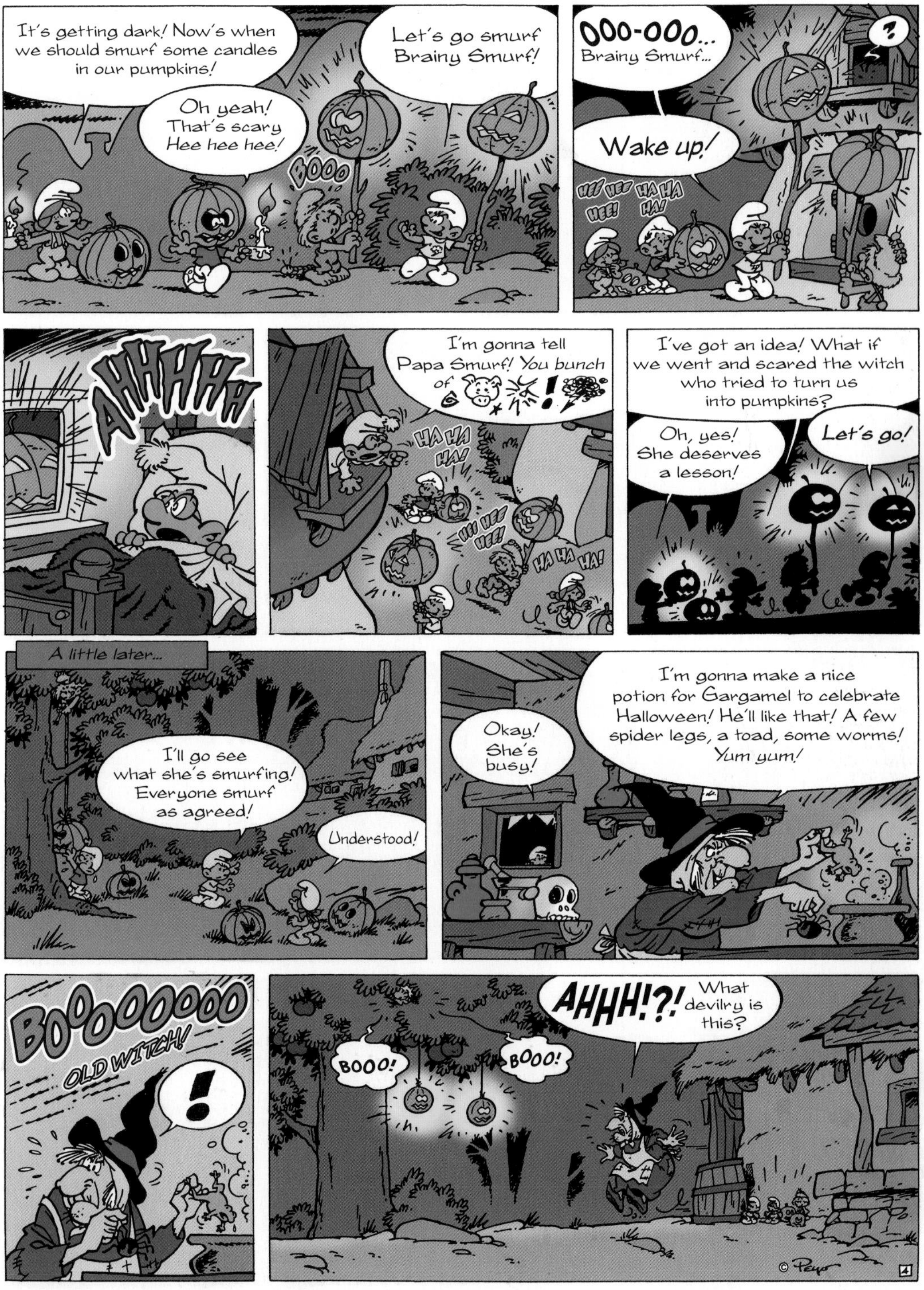

It's getting dark! Now's when we should smurf some candles in our pumpkins!
Oh yeah! That's scary Hee hee hee!
BOOO
Let's go smurf Brainy Smurf!
OOO-OOO... Brainy Smurf...
Wake up!
HEE HEE HEE!
HA HA HA!
?
AHHHHH
I'm gonna tell Papa Smurf! You bunch of
HA HA HA!
HEE HEE HEE!
HA HA HA!
I've got an idea! What if we went and scared the witch who tried to turn us into pumpkins?
Oh, yes! She deserves a lesson!
Let's go!
A little later...
I'll go see what she's smurfing! Everyone smurf as agreed!
Understood!
Okay! She's busy!
I'm gonna make a nice potion for Gargamel to celebrate Halloween! He'll like that! A few spider legs, a toad, some worms! Yum yum!
BOOOOOOOO
OLD WITCH!
!
AHHH!?!
What devilry is this?
BOOO!
BOOO!
© Peyo
4

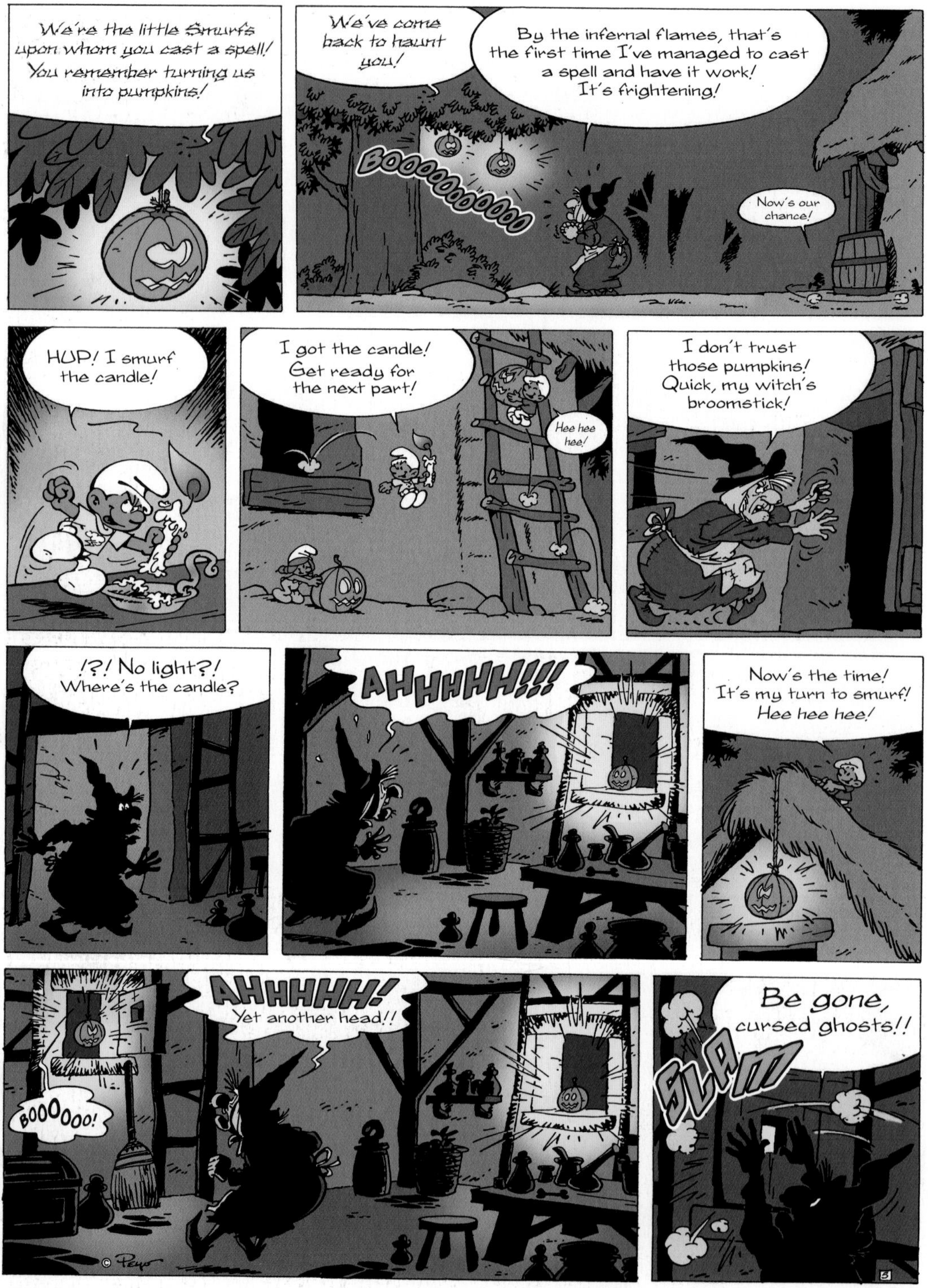
We're the little Smurfs upon whom you cast a spell! You remember turning us into pumpkins!
We've come back to haunt you!
By the infernal flames, that's the first time I've managed to cast a spell and have it work! It's frightening!
BOOOOOOOOOOOO
Now's our chance!
HUP! I smurf the candle!
I got the candle! Get ready for the next part!
Hee hee hee!
I don't trust those pumpkins! Quick, my witch's broomstick!
!?! No light?! Where's the candle?
AHHHHH!!!
Now's the time! It's my turn to smurf! Hee hee hee!
AHHHHH! Yet another head!!
BOOOOOO!
Be gone, cursed ghosts!!
SLAM
© Peyo
5

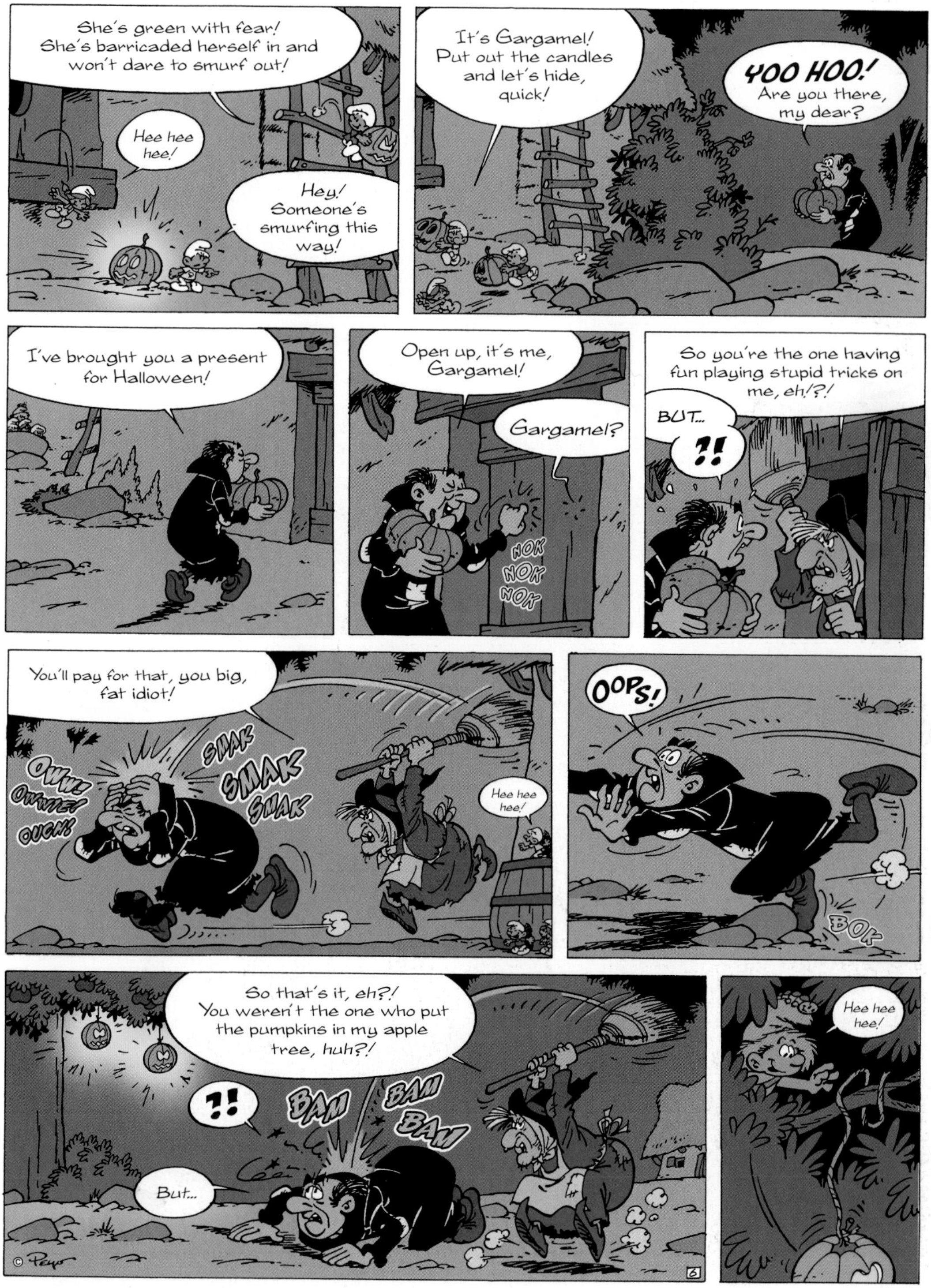

She's green with fear! She's barricaded herself in and won't dare to smurf out!
Hee hee hee!
Hey! Someone's smurfing this way!
It's Gargamel! Put out the candles and let's hide, quick!
YOO HOO! Are you there, my dear?
I've brought you a present for Halloween!
Open up, it's me, Gargamel!
Gargamel?
NOK NOK NOK
So you're the one having fun playing stupid tricks on me, eh!?!
BUT...
?!
You'll pay for that, you big, fat idiot!
OWW! OWWIE! OUCH!
SMAK SMAK SMAK
Hee hee hee!
OOPS!
BOK
So that's it, eh?! You weren't the one who put the pumpkins in my apple tree, huh?!
?!
BAM BAM BAM
But...
© Peyo
6
Hee hee hee!

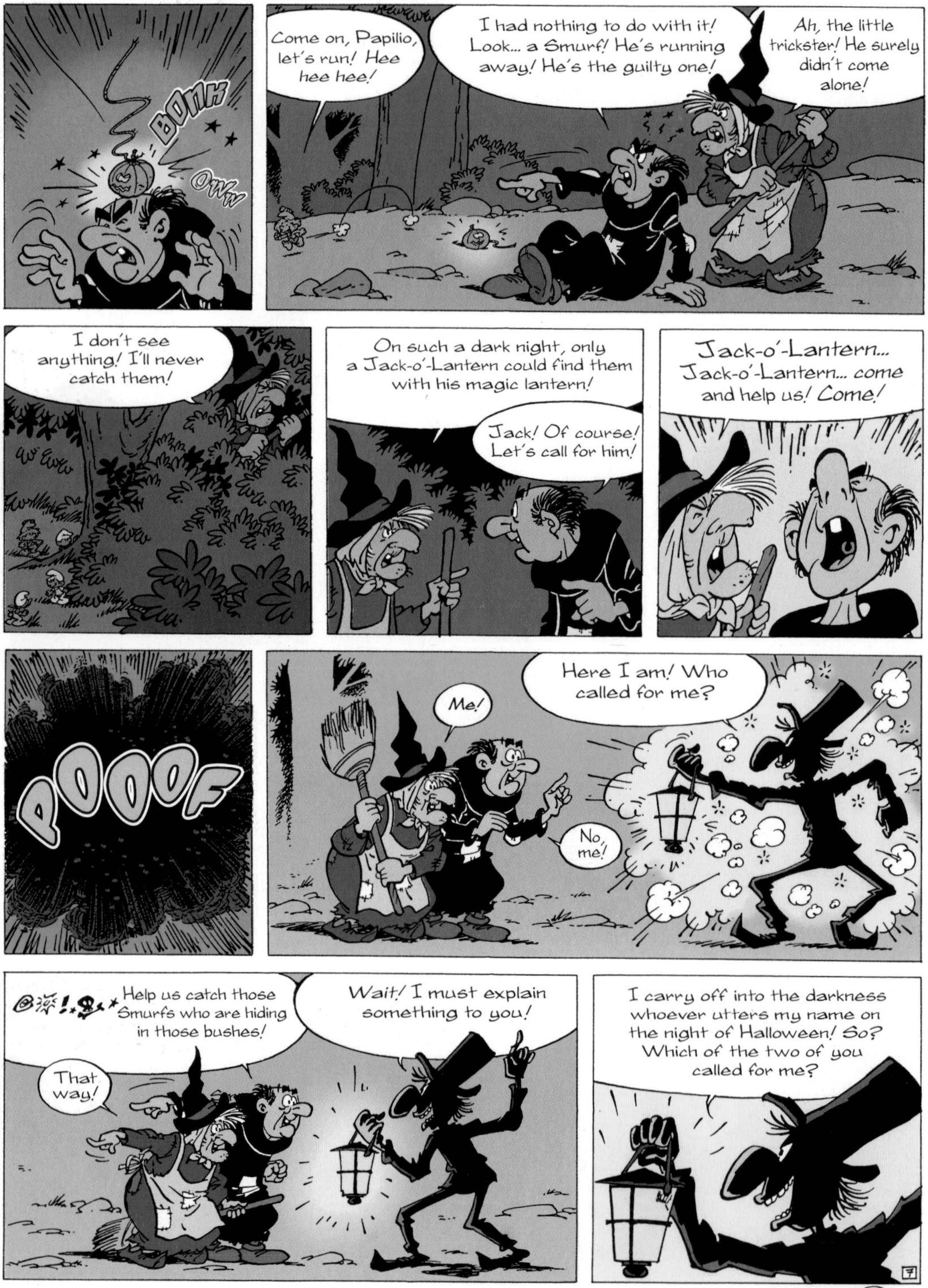

BONK
OWW
Come on, Papilio, let's run! Hee hee hee!
I had nothing to do with it! Look... a Smurf! He's running away! He's the guilty one!
Ah, the little trickster! He surely didn't come alone!
I don't see anything! I'll never catch them!
On such a dark night, only a Jack-o'-Lantern could find them with his magic lantern!
Jack! Of course! Let's call for him!
Jack-o'-Lantern... Jack-o'-Lantern... come and help us! Come!
POOOF
Here I am! Who called for me?
Me!
No, me!
Help us catch those Smurfs who are hiding in those bushes!
That way!
Wait! I must explain something to you!
I carry off into the darkness whoever utters my name on the night of Halloween! So? Which of the two of you called for me?
7
© Peyo

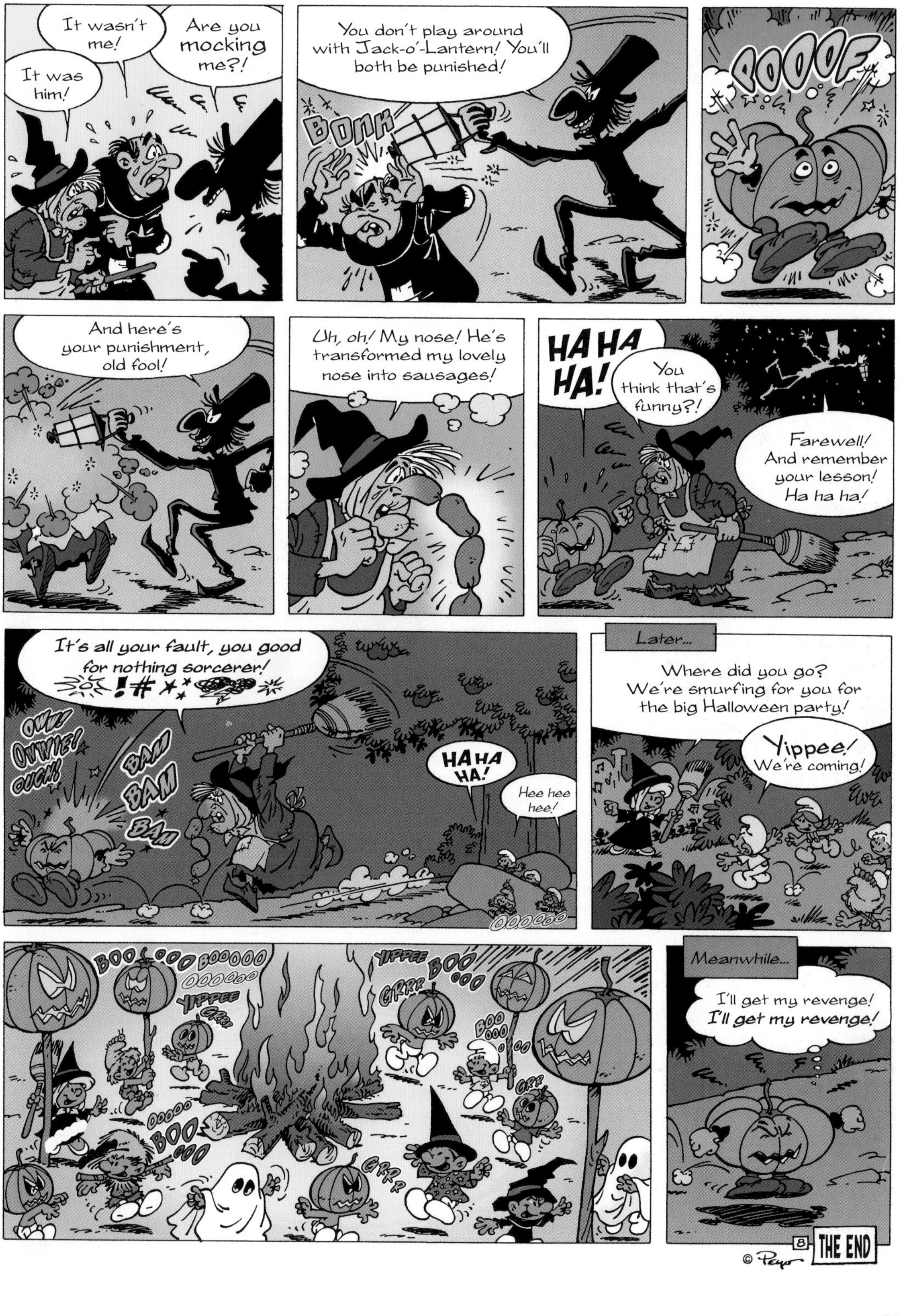
It was him!
It wasn't me!
Are you mocking me?!
You don't play around with Jack-o'-Lantern! You'll both be punished!
BONK
POOOF
And here's your punishment, old fool!
Uh, oh! My nose! He's transformed my lovely nose into sausages!
HA HA HA!
You think that's funny?!
Farewell! And remember your lesson! Ha ha ha!
It's all your fault, you good for nothing sorcerer!
OWW! OWWIE! OUCH!
BAM BAM BAM
HA HA HA!
Hee hee hee!
Later...
Where did you go? We're smurfing for you for the big Halloween party!
Yippee! We're coming!
BOOOOO BOOOOO
YIPPEE
GRRR
BOOOOO
Meanwhile...
I'll get my revenge! I'll get my revenge!
8
THE END
© Peyo

WATCH OUT FOR
PAPERCUT

Smurflator E. Joe Johnson

Welcome to the tear-jerking tenth SMURFS graphic novel by Peyo from Papercutz, the poetic and passionate publishers of great graphic novels for all ages. I'm Jim Salicrup, your hopelessly romantic Smurf-in-Chief. Ever since THE SMURFS #4 "The Smurfette" was published we've been bombarded with requests and outright demands for the return of the Smurfette! Even the Smurfs themselves were eager for her to return to the Smurf Village! Well, the long wait is over! The Smurfette's back, in all her smurfy glory! And we're not just talking about her starring role in the The Smurfs DVD, which features the Smurfs in their big-screen 3-D blockbuster! She's back in our pages where she belongs!

As you can see for yourself, where the Smurfette goes, trouble follows! That's why she left the Smurfs Village the first time. This time around she hasn't changed much—all she's asking for is the moon! (See what she missed by not being around during THE SMURFS #7 "The Astrosmurf"?) It also looks like she'll be sticking around a lot longer! In fact, she plays a very important role in THE SMURFS #11 "The Smurf Olympics," coming soon to booksellers everywhere.

And speaking of the lovable Smurfette, we should mention that like several other Papercutz graphic novel series, THE SMURFS were originally published in French—the language of love. Providing "smurflations" is none other than E. Joe Johnson. He is a Professor of French and Spanish and the chair of the Department of Humanities at Clayton State University in Metro Atlanta, Georgia. Pretty impressive, eh? He specializes in 18th-century French studies and has published five books, multiple scholarly articles, and scores of translations of French graphic novels for NBM Publishing and Papercutz. He thinks that working on THE SMURFS is pretty smurftastic.

We couldn't agree more with the good professor! We'd love to talk more about the Smurfs, but we're late for our appointment with our personal trainer! We're trying to get in shape for the Smurf Olympics! Smurf you later!

Jim

Smurf, always smurf.
Practice makes smurf.
For it's at the foot of the smurf that one smurfs the least.

Yes!

Everything smurfs to he who smurfs.

SMURFERIES

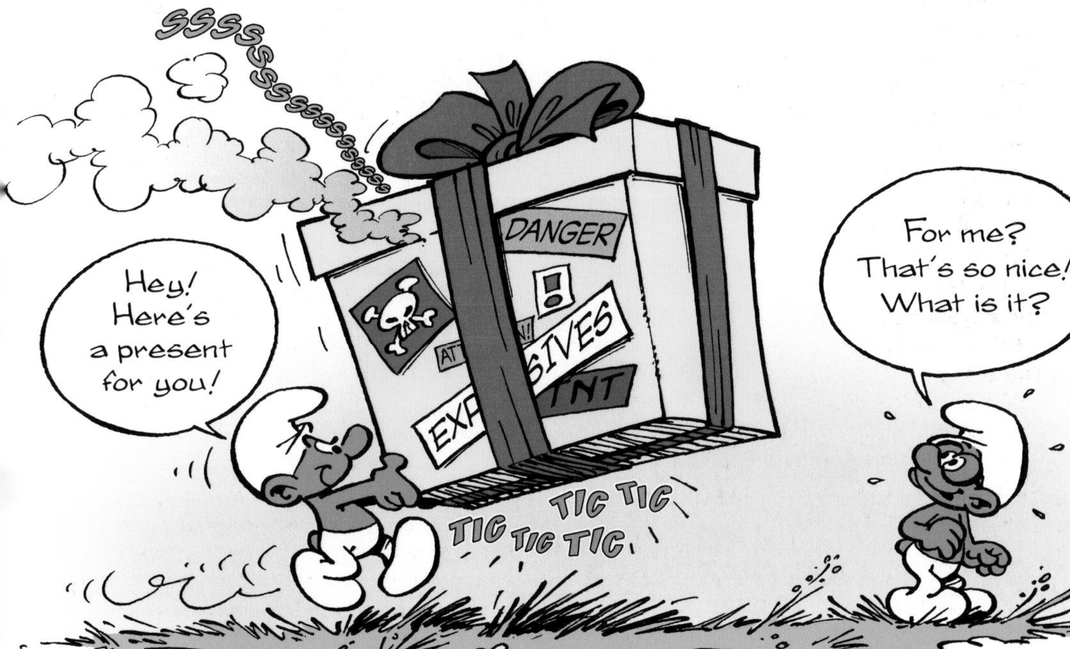

SSSSSSSSSSSSSSSSSS
Hey! Here's a present for you!
DANGER
ATT...N!
EXPLOSIVES
TNT
TIC TIC TIC TIC TIC
For me? That's so nice! What is it?

THERE ARE NONE SO SMURF AS THOSE WHO WILL NOT SMURF

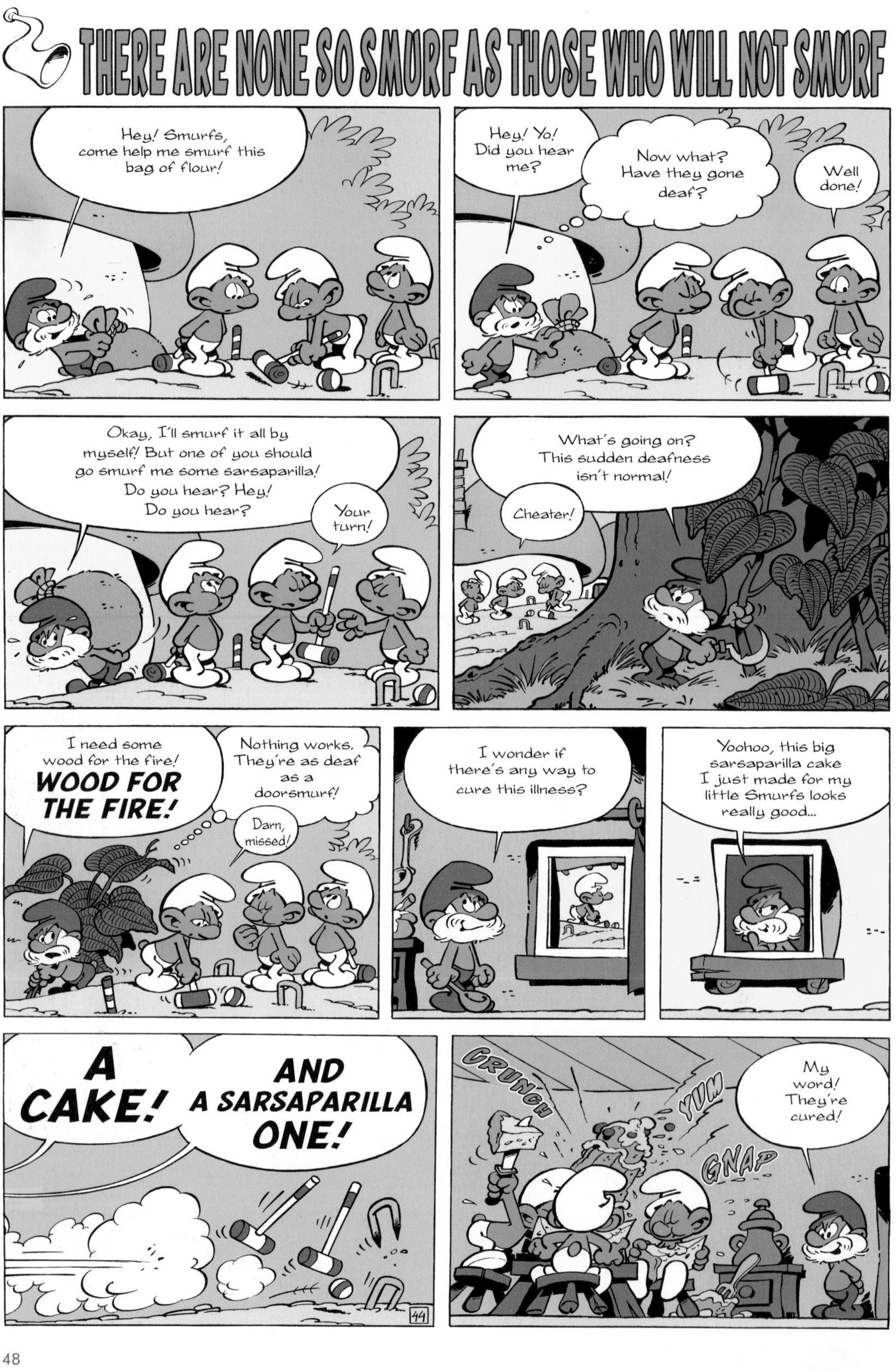
Hey! Smurfs, come help me smurf this bag of flour!
Hey! Yo! Did you hear me?
Now what? Have they gone deaf?
Well done!
Okay, I'll smurf it all by myself! But one of you should go smurf me some sarsaparilla! Do you hear? Hey! Do you hear?
Your turn!
What's going on? This sudden deafness isn't normal!
Cheater!
I need some wood for the fire! WOOD FOR THE FIRE!
Nothing works. They're as deaf as a doorsmurf!
Darn, missed!
I wonder if there's any way to cure this illness?
Yoohoo, this big sarsaparilla cake I just made for my little Smurfs looks really good...
A CAKE!
AND A SARSAPARILLA ONE!
44
CRUNCH
YUM
GNAP
My word! They're cured!

HOISTED ON HIS OWN SMURF

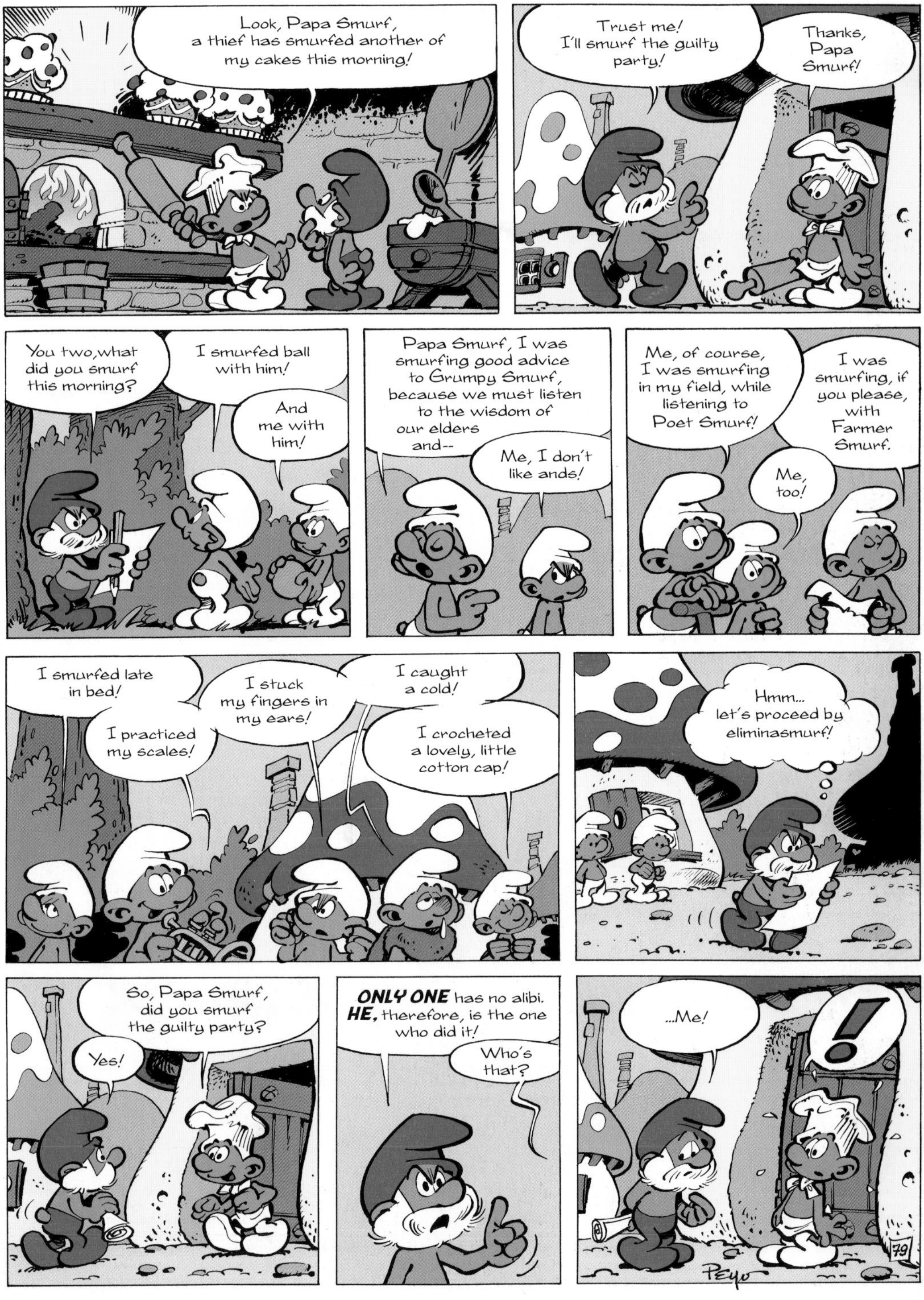

Look, Papa Smurf, a thief has smurfed another of my cakes this morning!
Trust me! I'll smurf the guilty party!
Thanks, Papa Smurf!
You two, what did you smurf this morning?
I smurfed ball with him!
And me with him!
Papa Smurf, I was smurfing good advice to Grumpy Smurf, because we must listen to the wisdom of our elders and--
Me, I don't like ands!
Me, of course, I was smurfing in my field, while listening to Poet Smurf!
Me, too!
I was smurfing, if you please, with Farmer Smurf.
I smurfed late in bed!
I practiced my scales!
I stuck my fingers in my ears!
I caught a cold!
I crocheted a lovely, little cotton cap!
Hmm... let's proceed by eliminasmurf!
So, Papa Smurf, did you smurf the guilty party?
Yes!
ONLY ONE has no alibi. **HE**, therefore, is the one who did it!
Who's that?
...Me!
!
79
PEYO

IT'S ALL FUN AND SMURFS, TILL SOMEONE GETS SMURFED

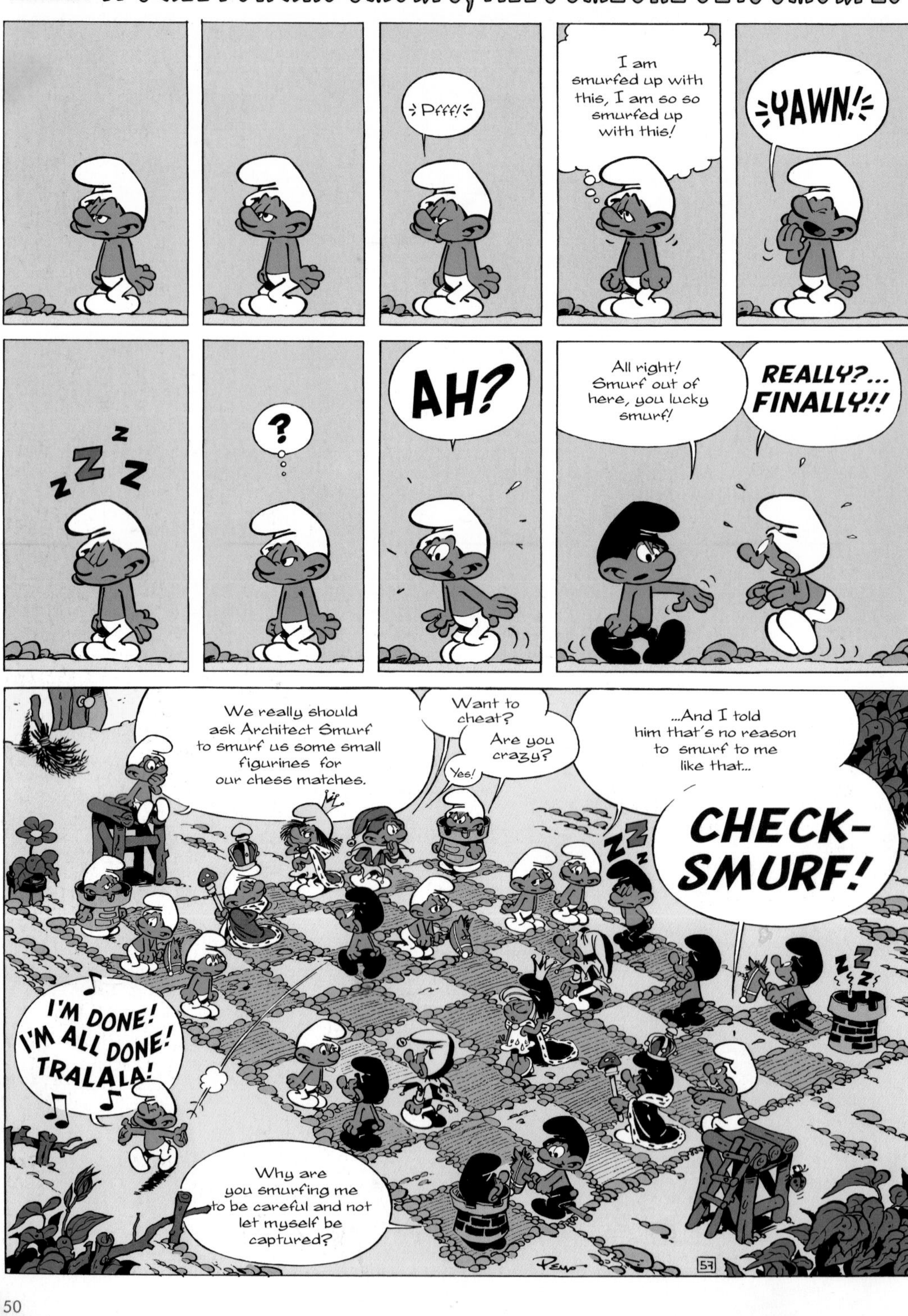
Pfff!
I am smurfed up with this, I am so so smurfed up with this!
YAWN!
Z Z Z Z
?
AH?
All right! Smurf out of here, you lucky smurf!
REALLY?... FINALLY!!
We really should ask Architect Smurf to smurf us some small figurines for our chess matches.
Want to cheat?
Are you crazy?
Yes!
...And I told him that's no reason to smurf to me like that...
CHECK-SMURF!
I'M DONE! I'M ALL DONE! TRALALA!
Why are you smurfing me to be careful and not let myself be captured?

DO NOT SMURF THE SMURF'S NAME IN VAIN...

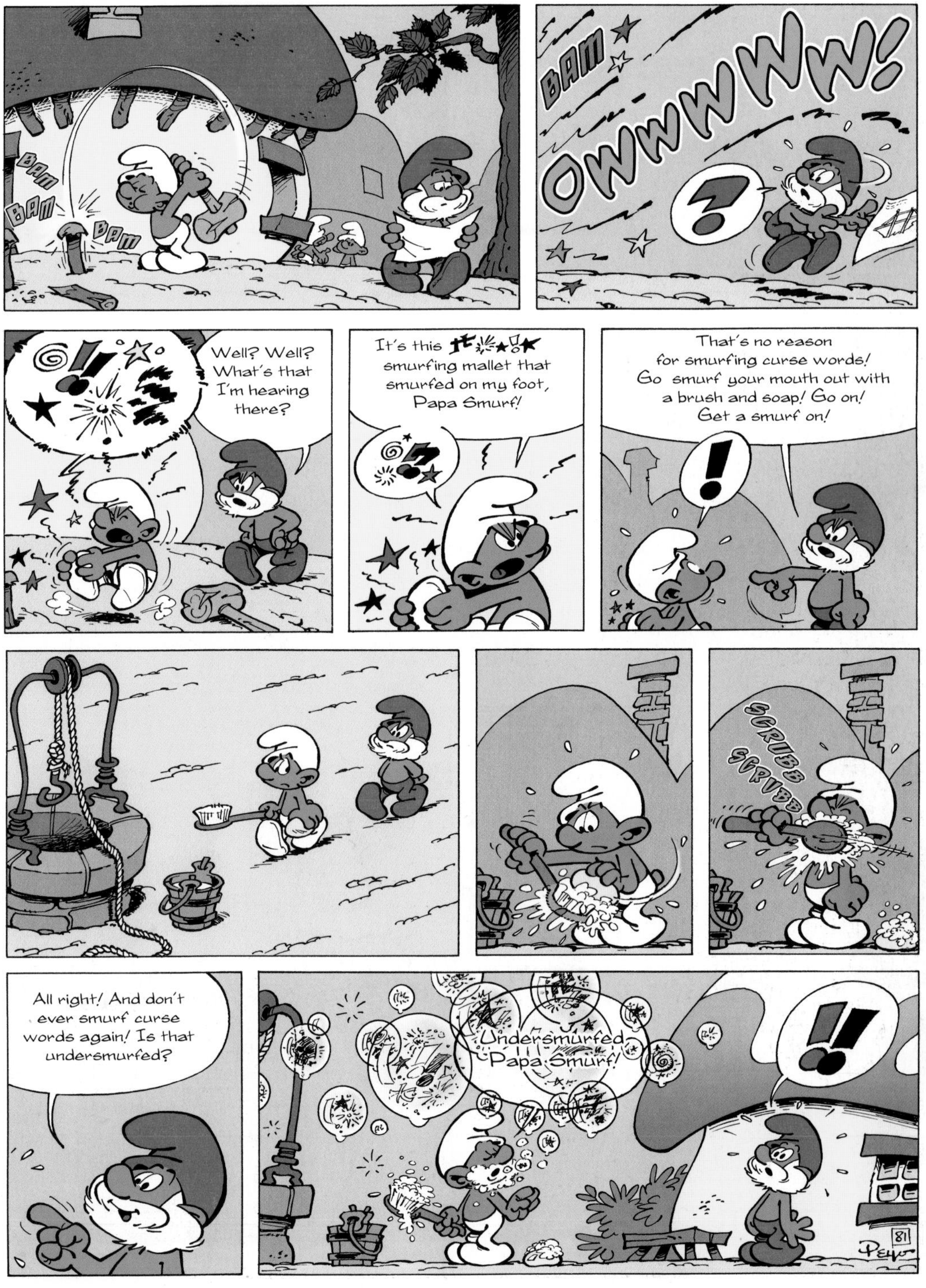

BAM
BAM
BAM
BAM
OWWWWW!
Well? Well? What's that I'm hearing there?
It's this smurfing mallet that smurfed on my foot, Papa Smurf!
That's no reason for smurfing curse words! Go smurf your mouth out with a brush and soap! Go on! Get a smurf on!
SCRUBB
SCRUBB
All right! And don't ever smurf curse words again! Is that undersmurfed?
Undersmurfed Papa Smurf!

STRIKE THE SMURF WHILE IT'S STILL SMURF

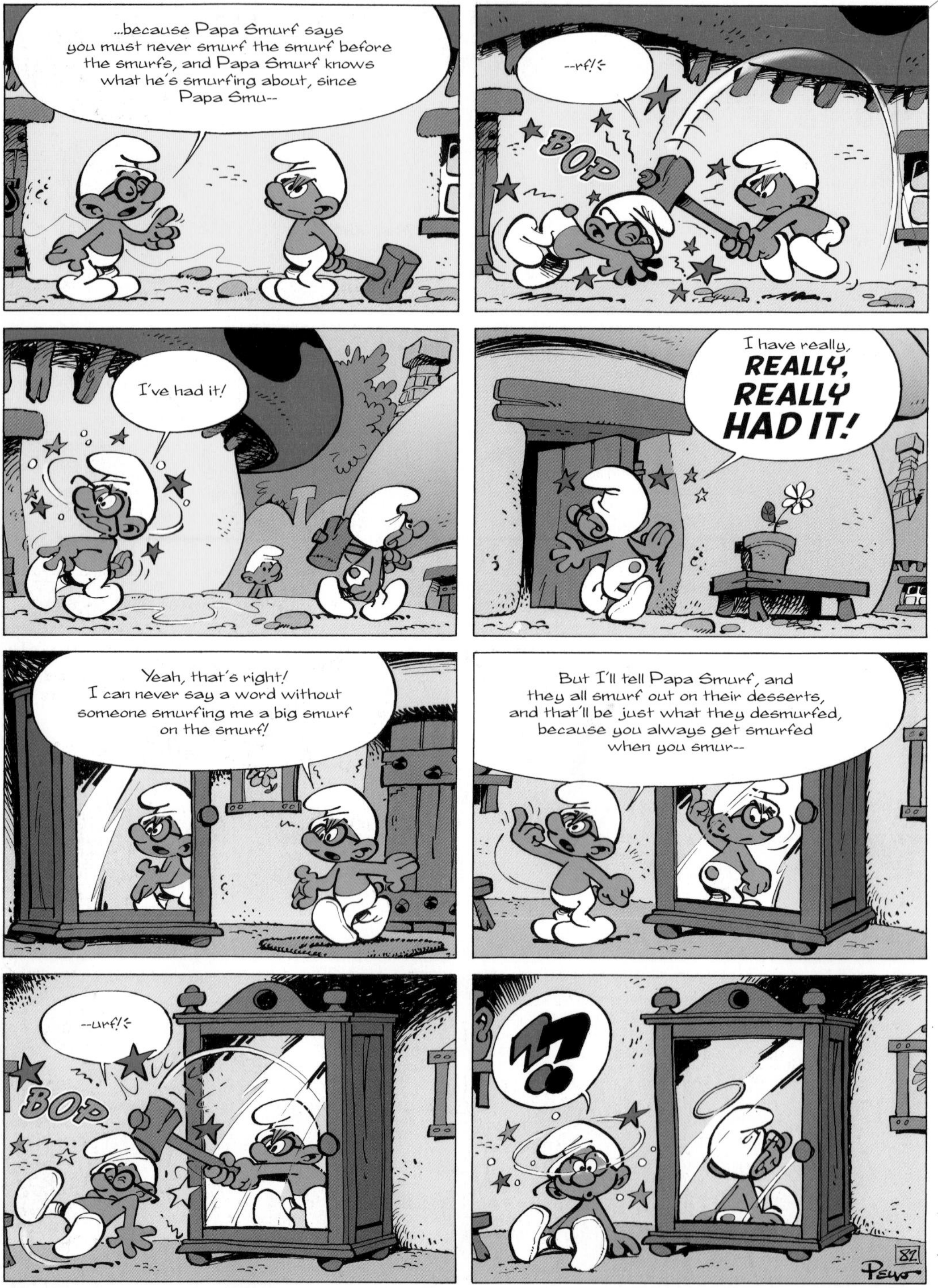

...because Papa Smurf says you must never smurf the smurf before the smurfs, and Papa Smurf knows what he's smurfing about, since Papa Smu--
--rf!
BOP
I've had it!
I have really, REALLY, REALLY HAD IT!
Yeah, that's right! I can never say a word without someone smurfing me a big smurf on the smurf!
But I'll tell Papa Smurf, and they all smurf out on their desserts, and that'll be just what they desmurfed, because you always get smurfed when you smur--
--urf!
BOP

SINGING IN THE SMURF

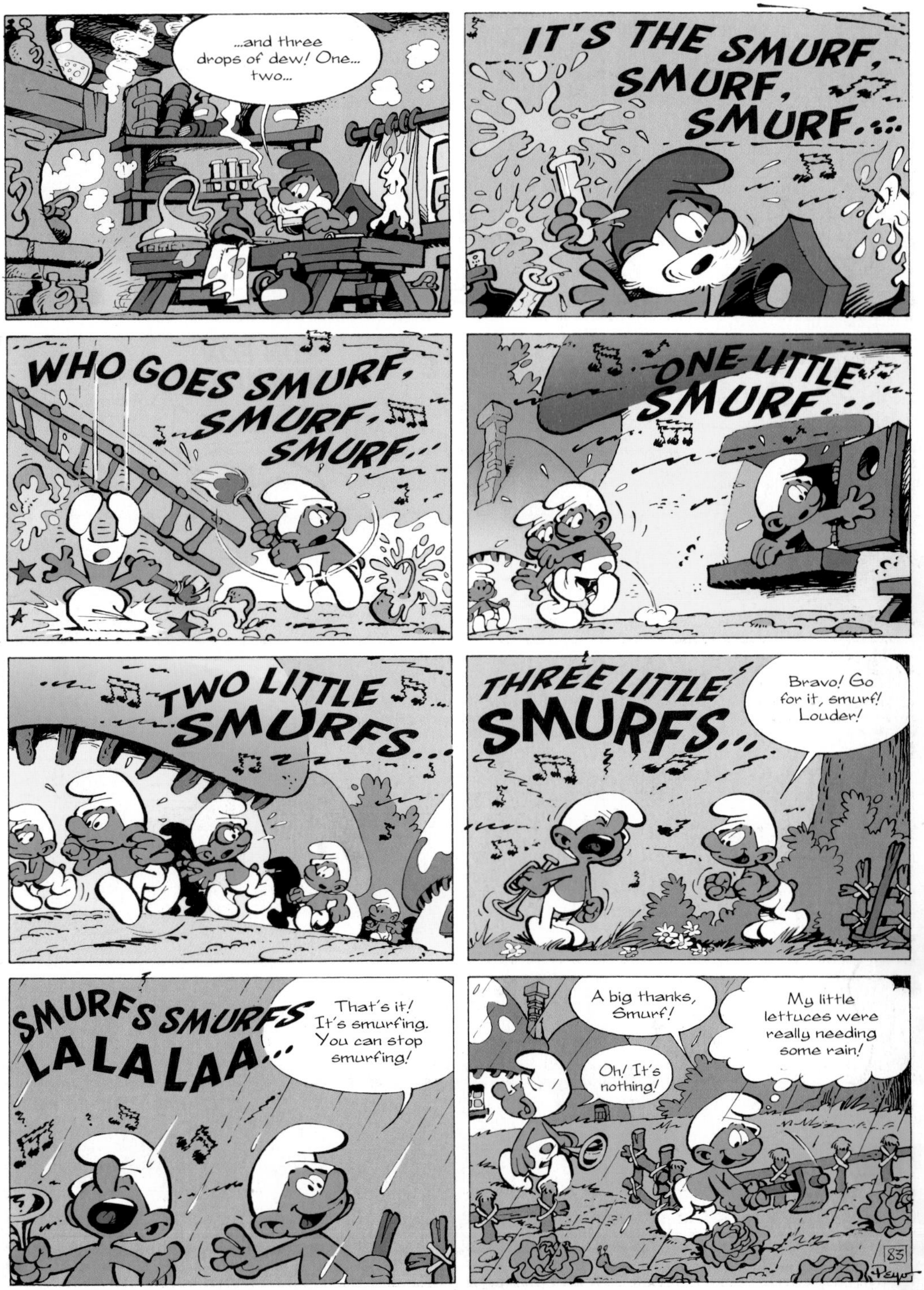
...and three drops of dew! One... two...
IT'S THE SMURF, SMURF, SMURF...
WHO GOES SMURF, SMURF, SMURF...
ONE LITTLE SMURF...
TWO LITTLE SMURFS...
THREE LITTLE SMURFS...
Bravo! Go for it, smurf! Louder!
SMURFS SMURFS LALALAA...
That's it! It's smurfing. You can stop smurfing!
A big thanks, Smurf!
Oh! It's nothing!
My little lettuces were really needing some rain!
83
Peyo

THERE'S NO SMURFCOUNTING FOR TASTE

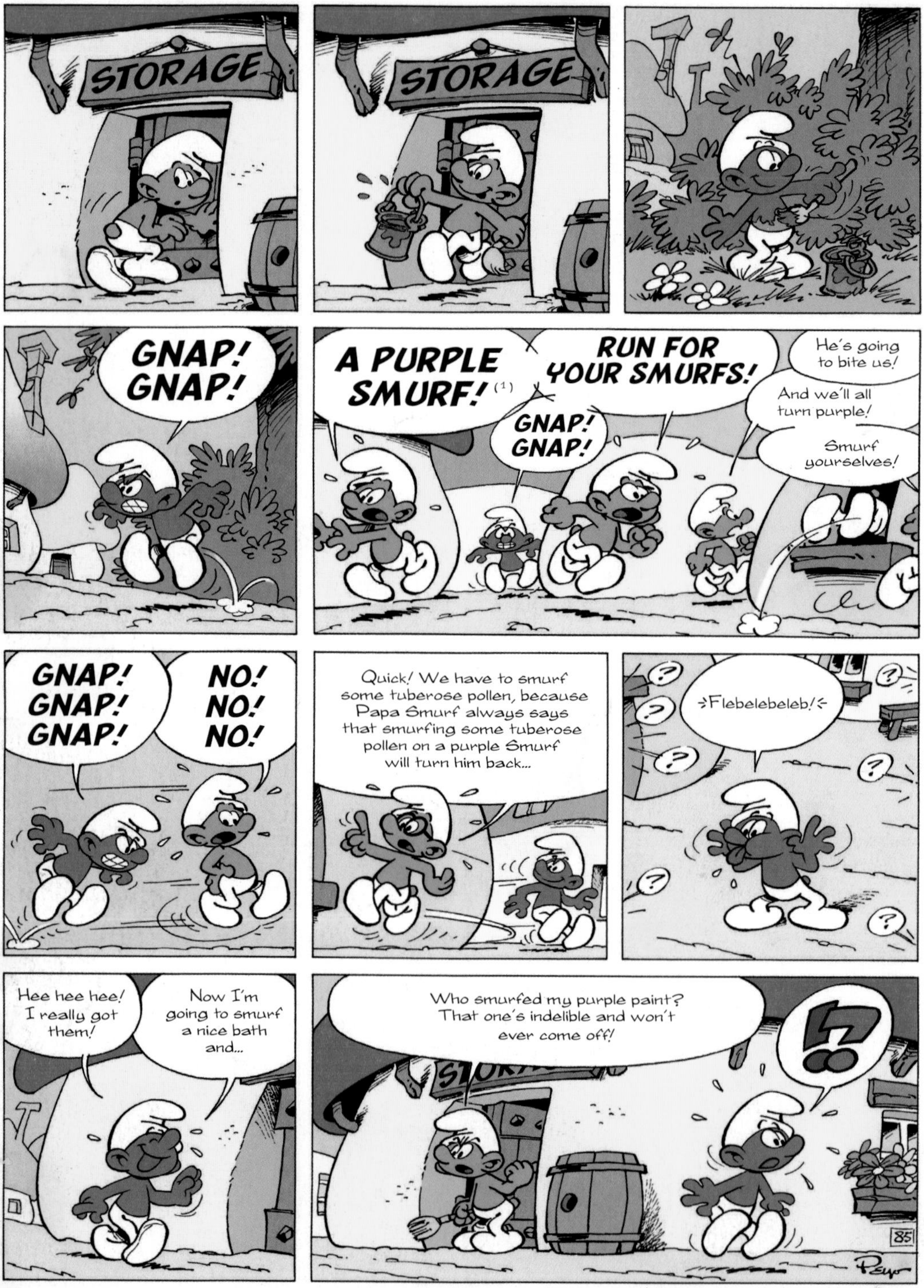
STORAGE
STORAGE
GNAP! GNAP!
A PURPLE SMURF! (1)
RUN FOR YOUR SMURFS!
GNAP! GNAP!
He's going to bite us!
And we'll all turn purple!
Smurf yourselves!
GNAP! GNAP! GNAP!
NO! NO! NO!
Quick! We have to smurf some tuberose pollen, because Papa Smurf always says that smurfing some tuberose pollen on a purple Smurf will turn him back...
Flebelebeleb!
Hee hee hee! I really got them!
Now I'm going to smurf a nice bath and...
Who smurfed my purple paint? That one's indelible and won't ever come off!
85

(1) See THE SMURFS #1 "The Purple Smurfs"

WHATEVER IS WELL-CONCEIVED CAN BE CLEARLY EXPLAINED

?
Hey? What's that smurf there?
It's a smurf!
Oh? What's it smurf for?
Well, for smurfing!
For smurfing what?
Some smurf with smurf!
Really? And how does it smurf?
It's simple! You smurf on this smurf, and the smurf smurfs into smurf!
And if you smurf on this other smurf, do you smurf some smurfed smurfs?
Ah, no!
Why?
Because the smurf is smurfed for smurfing smurf with smurf and not smurfed smurfs.
Ah?
But if you smurfed on the two smurfs at the same time?
Don't ever smurf that, you'd smurf the whole thing!
Smurf closely to me, I'm going to smurf you how this smurf smurfs! You see this smurf here?
Yes!
Okay! Well, when you smurf on this smurf, you're smurfing a series of smurfed intersmurfed between them, which, by desmurfing, smurf by the smurf some smurf to smurf! Do you smurf?
Yes, yes!
He doesn't seem like he undersmurfed! But that was clear, wasn't it?
86

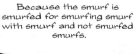

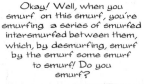

DRESSING FOR SMURFCESS

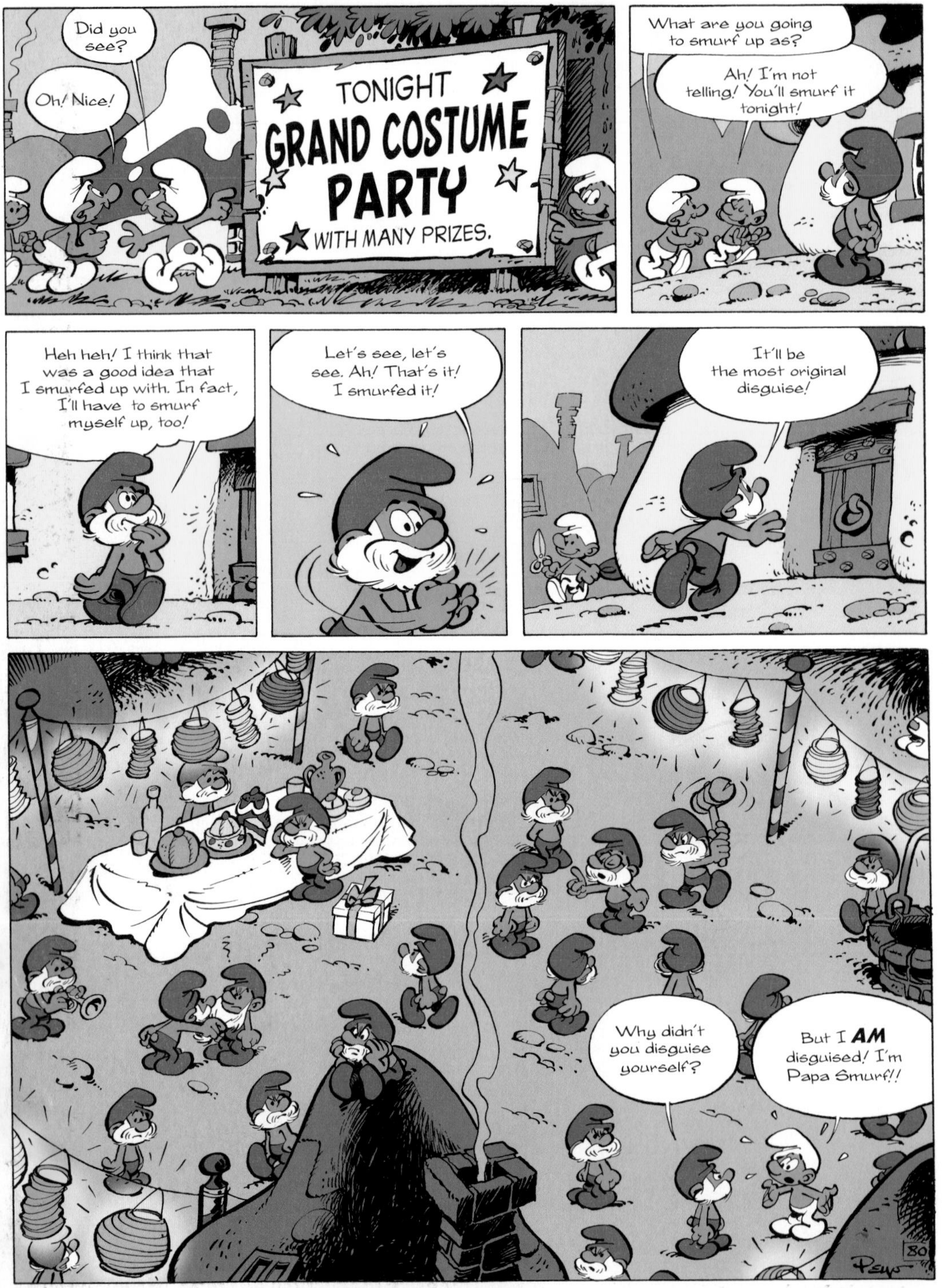

Did you see?
Oh! Nice!
TONIGHT
GRAND COSTUME PARTY
WITH MANY PRIZES.
What are you going to smurf up as?
Ah! I'm not telling! You'll smurf it tonight!
Heh heh! I think that was a good idea that I smurfed up with. In fact, I'll have to smurf myself up, too!
Let's see, let's see. Ah! That's it! I smurfed it!
It'll be the most original disguise!
Why didn't you disguise yourself?
But I AM disguised! I'm Papa Smurf!!
80
Peyo